Grimmtastic Girls

Snowflake Freezes Up

Grimmtastic Girls

Grimmtastic Girls
Snowflake Freezes Up

Joan Holub & Suzanne Williams

Scholastic Inc.

ISBN 978-0-545-94534-9

10 9 8 7 6 5 4 3   16 17 18 19 20

Printed in the U.S.A.   40
First printing 2016
Book design by Yaffa Jaskoll

For our grimmtastic readers:

Madelyn B., Christine D-H., Khanya S., Julia K., Annie J., Tessa M., Alexandria M., Megan D., Abby-Grace G., Gina P., Jolee S., Jenna S., Sarah S., Amanda H., Danielle T., Emily C., Ava K., Kaitlyn W., Cheyanne W., Kristen S., Alyssa B., Clara B., Stacey B., Becca S., Avery S., Morgan S., Arabella V., Ashlyn C., Cheng X., Huay X., Niharika P., Allie B., Jayla M., Sara B., Hailey H., Amelia G., Caitlin R., Hannah R., Emma T., Ally M., Keyra M., Sabrina C. — and you!

— JH and SW

Contents

It is written upon the wall of the Grimmstone Library:

Something E.V.I.L. this way comes.
To protect all that is born of fairy-tale, folktale, and nursery-
rhyme magic, we have created the realm of Grimmlandia. In
the center of this realm, we have built two castles on opposite
ends of a Great Hall, which straddles the Once Upon River. And
this haven shall be forever known as Grimm Academy.

~The brothers Grimm

1
Jack Frost

$\mathcal{I}$t was Thursday morning, and Jack Frost was in a snit as usual. In fact, he was totally frosted! Because it was *sooo* boring in Snow Globe Town, the miniature village that filled the beach ball–size snow globe he lived inside at Grimm Academy.

A snowman stood at the very center of the village. Tired of its jolly, empty-headed grin, Jack whipped the snowman's black hat off and stomped up and down on it with his pointy-toed boots. Then he kicked the fake fir tree nearby and did a double backflip before flitting around the snow globe's tiny buildings.

How dare Jacob and Wilhelm Grimm imprison him in here? Jack thought for the frostzillionth time. He stuck out an elbow and knocked an icicle off one of the cute houses in Snow Globe Town as he drifted by. Trapped inside this globe, he could only float among the teeny snowflakes day after day like a goldfish in a wintry bowl.

Those two brothers had stuck him in here around the same time they'd brought other characters from literature to Grimm Academy for safekeeping. But unlike Jack, those other characters from fairy tales, folktales, and nursery rhymes all roamed free. Which wasn't fair! He'd spent far too many years inside this globe on this shelf in Grimmstone Library's Crystal Room, surrounded by crystal balls and lots of crystal statuary. Talk about dullsville!

But he was making plans, plotting the mischief he'd cause when he got out one day. He only hoped that day would come soon.

Suddenly, Jack Frost heard the door to the Crystal Room open. Without warning, two scaly green hands shot toward him, grabbing his glass prison. The hands belonged to a dragon lady! She shook the globe, rocking his world. Flakes of snow around him became a white flurry as he went flying to and fro.

"Frabjous! I could use an extra-large paperweight," cackled the dragon lady. "This snow globe is perfect."

Next thing Jack knew, he and his fake village had been relocated to the Academy office to steady a bunch of flyaway papers on the lady's desk. He quickly figured out that she was the principal's assistant, Ms. Jabberwocky.

Sitting day after boring day on a shelf in the library had been bad enough, but to serve as a *paperweight*? He, who had the power to bring frigid, wintry days? The power to frost the ground so people would slip and slide? Oh, the indignity of it all. And what a stupendous waste of his talents!

Fuming, Jack Frost plotted his revenge. Should he ever get free, he would waste no time in locating the wickedest character at Grimm Academy. From what he had overheard from snippets of conversation between students who'd occasionally wandered into the Crystal Room over the years, that character would be the very vain, extremely evil Ms. Wicked. She was also the Scrying — as in crystal-ball gazing and fortune-telling — teacher at GA.

He would offer to be her sidekick. When they joined forces, they would rule! Well, mostly he'd be the one ruling if he had his way.

As the morning of his relocation passed, Jack perked up. This outer office was the nerve center for the entire Academy! It turned out that he had a great view of the goings-on from his new perch atop Ms. Jabberwocky's desk. Late that afternoon, a bunch of students came to see her. While they were there, the office door opened and in walked trouble.

"Troll Moving Company. Where are the mirrors you want moved to the Grimmstone Library?" asked a sturdy-looking troll wearing a uniform.

Ms. Jabberwocky waved him toward the inner office, where the principal's door stood. "In there. And the sooner Ms. Wicked's possessions are gone, the better. Thank grimmness we've seen the last of her!"

The thick glass of the snow globe muffled sound. However, Jack Frost had gotten good at guessing what people were saying by reading their lips if they were close enough. At the moment, the trolls and the dragon lady were nearby, so doing this was easy.

Huh? he thought now in dismay. He must be behind in the news. Last he'd heard, Ms. Wicked had taken over the job as principal of the school when Principal Rumpelstiltskin went missing. What was going on here?

He didn't have to wait long to find out. As the trolls promptly set to work removing the mirrors and lugging them into the hall, the principal came out of his office. When had *he* returned to Grimm Academy?

A dark-haired girl among the group of students was called into the principal's office. Something about spinning straw into gold? For a while afterward, there were too many people around to tell who was saying what or going where.

Suddenly, all went dark. Ms. Jabberwocky had just buried his snow globe under some papers. *Thanks a lot, lady!*

Now he couldn't see a thing. And though he strained to hear, the papers muted the sounds around him.

"What's happening?" he demanded, banging his little fists against the inside of the globe in frustration. But he wasn't surprised when nobody answered. No one could hear him through the thick glass.

Crash! What was that? It sounded to him like a mirror had broken. The very next moment, something bumped his globe, sending it flying. It landed on the office floor, then rolled crazily off into a corner, where (annoyingly) he still couldn't see anything. He sat there, feeling dizzy from all the commotion.

Hey! A crack had formed in his snow globe, Jack noticed with excitement. Must have happened when it hit the floor.

At last, a way out!

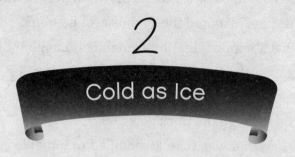

2

Cold as Ice

Fifteen minutes earlier . . .

At the end of sixth-period class on Thursday, twelve-year-old Snowflake was summoned to her doom. In other words, she got called to the principal's office.

She'd been to the office only once before — a week ago when she'd first enrolled at Grimm Academy — to get her class assignments. Going there again was something she'd rather avoid. Why? Because she was afraid of fire-breathing dragons. And the office assistant, Ms. Jabberwocky, was the closest thing there was to a dragon that she'd ever met.

She dropped off her Handbook in her trunker, which was the same as a locker except it was an actual trunk standing on end along the hall. Reflected in the mirror that hung inside her trunker's door, Snowflake's heart-shaped face looked pale against her long, shiny black hair. The ends of her hair looked as if they'd been dipped in blue ink, but it was naturally that way, not dyed.

After shutting her trunker, Snowflake stepped over to a nearby window. The glass was a little foggy. She drew a little round peephole in the misty pane with her fingertip so she could peek outside. Back when she was a little girl in her village, the grandmother who ran the orphanage she'd grown up in had shown her how to do that.

A pang of homesickness filled her. She pushed it away. She could not go back to the village on the outskirts of Grimmlandia, not ever. Her old friends were scared of her now. Scared of her powers. She'd overheard them gossiping that she was being sent here to GA for "observation." Whether or not that was true, she had no idea. However, she didn't like the thought of being spied on, especially since, lately, things around her could sometimes get, well, *weird*.

Hearing footsteps, Snowflake glanced over her shoulder and saw a boy she didn't recognize heading in her direction. Hoping he hadn't seen her looking his way, she started off again, walking fast now. As she moved ahead of him down the first-floor hall of Grimm Academy, she pretended to study the interior of the building, trying to appear totally fascinated by her surroundings. And she was, actually. But she was also hoping the boy wouldn't speak to her if she looked busy.

She adored the Academy. Especially its architecture. She was really into buildings. However, although she was really good at designing cool ones on paper, she was no good at figuring out their internal structure — their bones. Everything she had ever actually built for real tended to fall down. Luckily, she hadn't built this school!

Her admiring gaze noted the marble walls here in Pink Castle. They were the pale pink of a morning sunrise and were hung with tapestries stitched with scenes of elaborate feasts and pageantry. Tall stone support columns, whose tops were carved with birds, flowers, and gargoyles, supported the high ceilings.

At the other end of the school was Gray Castle, so-called because of its blue-gray walls. A Great Hall stretched between the two castles like a multistory bridge across the bright blue waters of the Once Upon River, which flowed merrily along underneath. Boys lived in dorms atop Gray Castle and girls lived in dorms atop Pink Castle, but they all shared classes on the lower floors of both castles during the day.

"Hey, do you know where the principal's office is?"

Quibblesnorts! That boy had caught up with her. He was tall and had wavy dark brown hair and green eyes. He also looked fit, like a guy who'd be good at sports.

"On the fourth floor of Pink Castle," Snowflake replied. "Up the grand staircase with the other offices and stuff." After sharing that information, she sped up.

"The grand where-case?" he asked, easily keeping pace with her.

Was that supposed to be a joke? She was in no mood. She sighed and slowed down a little. Maybe he'd go ahead of her and she could drop back even more. No such luck. He stuck with her, gazing around the halls with interest, too.

So why had he been called to the office? she wondered. For that matter, why had *she* been called? She couldn't be in academic trouble already, could she? Was this about that failing grade she'd gotten on her very first Comportment test? That was a dumb class about manners. The teacher, Ms. Queenharts, should be nicknamed Ms. Meanharts if she'd reported that grade to the principal before Snowflake even had a chance to try to do better!

Thing was, she'd never been good at tests. If she even heard the word *test*, she got instant brain freeze. So she'd panicked when Ms. Queenharts had announced a pop quiz yesterday. The quiz had been about cutlery arrangements for fancy occasions. Unable to think straight, Snowflake had gotten the correct placement of knives, forks, and spoons completely reversed.

Though she was pretty sure she wasn't dim-witted, she knew that some kids at her old school — and probably here now, too — thought she wasn't the brightest candle in the candelabra. And sometimes her frustration during tests made her feel, well, *testy*. Twice at her old school she'd gotten so flustered that she'd stormed out of a classroom in the middle of a quiz. Still, she'd never admit she had a problem.

She tried to act tough. She *was* tough. Cold as ice. Didn't need anybody or anything. That was her. The new her, anyway. Because if you didn't let anyone get close enough to make friends, no one could hurt your feelings, right? She'd been hurt in the past, betrayed by her so-called friends in the village. But she didn't want to think about that right now.

Just then, she reached the grand staircase and began to climb.

"So, is the office up these stairs?" the boy asked. When she nodded curtly, he turned to follow her up. Now they walked side by side, the only ones on the stairs, not speaking. Despite her vow to be tough, the silence was starting to get uncomfortable.

"You going to the office, too?" he asked.

She nodded again, but without looking his way. "Mm-hmm."

"Think we're going to be fried?" he asked.

"Huh?" Now she did look at him. Was he scared of dragons, too?

He grinned, one side of his mouth quirking up just a little higher than the other to cause a dimple in his cheek.

"I'm a little jittery about the alchemy experiments. Back home at my school, we heard rumors about this place. Something about a grumpy principal? And students getting melted into lumps during his gold-making experiments? I even heard that Principal Rumpelstiltskin —"

Snowflake stopped dead on the second-floor landing. "Ooh! Don't ever call him that!" she said automatically, her blue eyes going round. "I've only been here a week, but even I know that's a really bad idea. It's against the rules, and he'll get super upset."

All of this was information she'd figured out on her own or looked up in the Academy Handbook. Although everything had been new to her when she'd arrived at GA, she'd never asked anyone for help. That could lead to making friends.

"So what do I call him?" the boy asked as they continued upward again. "Does he use a nickname?"

She shot him another glance. She supposed she should try to help him. He might not be as skilled as she was at figuring stuff out. "Mostly, Principal R."

"His nickname is Mostly Principal R?"

"No —" Thinking he'd misunderstood, Snowflake started to explain that he should leave off the *mostly*. But then she noticed his eyes were twinkling. He'd been joking around. "Oh," she said.

He laughed, sending light gold sparkles into his green eyes. "Maybe we should make up our own nicknames for him," the boy went on. "Like Principal Rumpelgold. Or how about Rumpygrumpy? Or Grumpystiltskin?"

She laughed, too, now, though her laugh sounded a bit rusty since she hadn't used it in a while. "That last one's already a nickname the students call him."

"Okay, Crankystiltskin, instead," the boy said as they reached the third floor. They both laughed again.

"The guys at my old school would think it was hilarious to hear me say I'm freaked out about meeting him," he confided. "I'm considered kind of a tough guy back home."

Snowflake stared at him. She was tough, too, or trying to be. It surprised her that he might be like her.

She let down her guard a little more, and soon, they were talking away like they'd known each other for weeks.

"You're new?" she asked him.

He nodded. "Just got here a few minutes ago by coach. I'm supposed to get my class assignments and trunker key from the office first thing according to a letter I was sent."

"I came last Friday," she told him. They'd arrived at the top of the grand staircase on the fourth floor. To their left was a door. When he reached out for its knob, she moved quicker and had the door open first. Beyond it, a twisty staircase to their right went up to the fifth- and sixth-floor girls' dorms, but she took him past those stairs and down the hall instead. "This way. The office is down here."

As they headed through the hall, they passed a door that was propped open. She looked in and saw it was the library. For some reason, there were a bunch of sturdy-looking trolls wearing uniforms in there talking to Ms. Goose, the librarian.

The boy beside her craned his neck, noticing the rows and rows of books and other stuff visible through the doorway. "The library?" he asked.

"Mm-hmm. It moves around the Academy, though, so it probably won't be here tomorrow."

"Yeah?" He looked a little skeptical.

She nodded. "Cross my heart. It's true. Just look for a plain brass doorknob along the halls next time you need to find it. It could be anywhere in the school, but you'll know it because it's the only knob that doesn't have the intertwined GA logo on it. There's more to tell about the library, but I don't want to overwhelm you."

"Too late! I'm already overwhelmed," he told her. But his smile showed that he didn't really mean it.

So far, Snowflake had successfully kept her distance from other students at GA, but this boy's smile made her want to smile back. She wondered who he was and whether he was a character from a fairy tale or a nursery rhyme or what. But she didn't ask since she didn't want him asking her the same thing. Because she didn't have an answer.

The grandmother at the orphanage had informed her she was probably from a nursery rhyme. It hadn't seemed to matter to anyone *which* rhyme until lately, when her so-called "powers" had started to become a problem.

Snowflake was sure that once this boy got to know the real her and found out what a troublemaker she was (just ask anyone in her village), he wouldn't like her. She steeled herself not to care. She didn't need anyone to like her. She didn't need friends. Certainly not the kind from her village who ratted you out when your magic powers started to make themselves known.

"This is it," she said. They'd arrived at the office.

When they started to go in, the boy stopped and touched the top of his head. "Uh-oh. Forgot my crown back in my luggage. I'd better go catch the footmen before they stick my bags in a room somewhere."

"Oh. You're a prince?" she asked.

He nodded. Reading her startled expression, he seemed to misinterpret it. Quickly, he added, "I'm not trying to show off with the crown. It's just that I promised my parents I'd wear it when I officially meet the principal."

There were lots of princes and princesses here at GA. When new students enrolled, especially royalty like this boy, she'd heard there was often a ball to celebrate. There'd been no fanfare or big announcement upon her arrival, though. Probably wouldn't have been even if she'd been a princess. Because when she'd first come to GA, Principal R had been missing, so no one had been feeling very festive.

The boy headed back down the hall the way they'd come. After a half-dozen steps, he turned so he was walking backward away from her. "So what's your name? What fairy tale are you from?"

"Good luck finding that crown. See you!" she said, speaking over him.

He sent her a surprised, almost-hurt look. However, Snowflake gave him the cold shoulder so as to avoid having to admit she had no idea how to answer his question. She'd been dropped on the orphanage doorstep without a clue as to her identity. It had been snowing that day, so the grandmother had simply named her Snowflake. And the name had stuck.

The instant the boy turned away, she regretted that she hadn't explained at least a little of her story to him. But she'd waited a few seconds too long. By now he was too far away for her to say anything without yelling. With a regretful shrug, Snowflake stepped through the door into the office.

3

Crack!

The office was bustling, filled with other students who all seemed to be talking to Ms. Jabberwocky about Scrying. That was a class where they were supposed to use crystal balls and mirrors to look into the future. Snowflake had it fourth period. But since the Scrying teacher, Ms. Wicked, had escaped to avoid banishment right before Snowflake had arrived at GA, they'd just had study hall all week.

Before Snowflake could find out what was going on here exactly, the trolls from the library walked in. She got pushed aside and wound up standing next to two Grimm girls, Rose (aka Sleeping Beauty) and Snow White. Although Snowflake had kept to herself all week, her eyes and ears had been open, and she'd learned a lot about who was who around here.

"Troll Moving Company," the head troll announced to Ms. Jabberwocky. "You summoned us?"

"Callooh! Callay! Yes, I've been ex*pect*ing you," the principal's assistant told the trolls. She had a language all her own, and when she'd pronounced the letter *p,* a bit of fire had sputtered out of her nostrils.

Snowflake tensed and glanced toward the door to the hall, ready to run if the whole place went up in flames. Luckily, Prince Knightly, who was Rose's crush, stepped on the bit of fire. It fizzled out on the floor under his boot.

Meanwhile, Ms. Jabberwocky was waving the movers into another smaller office beyond this one. The sign on its door read: PRINCIPAL R'S OFFICE.

"Please cover and remove all the mirrors from the principal's office. Store them in the library, in Section *M* for mirrors," she instructed.

"Good! That ought to stop Ms. Wicked from coming back to the Academy through one of those mirrors," Snowflake heard Rose murmur to Snow White.

"Yeah. We're better off with her in the Nothingterror . . . or wherever she ended up," Snow White replied. The Dark Nothingterror was an awful place outside the realm, so it was kind of surprising Snow White felt that way. After all, Ms. Wicked was her stepmom!

When the trolls promptly began taking Ms. Wicked's mirrors away from the principal's office, Snow White glanced at Snowflake. The girl must have seen her puzzled look, because she added, "My stepmom was a member of E.V.I.L. That's —"

"Exceptional Villains in Literature?" Snowflake interrupted before Snow White could finish explaining. "Yeah, I know about them. News that big has spread to every village in the realm by now, I expect."

Rumor was that the mysterious and villainous society had existed around the time the two Grimm brothers had penned their fairy-tale books. But it had later died out. For some reason, it had begun to operate again in recent months. And it seemed bent on weakening the magical wall around Grimmlandia that had kept all the fairy-tale, nursery-rhyme, and other literary characters within its borders safe for more than a century. Since Snowflake had come to GA, she'd also heard rumors about a counter organization some students had begun called G.O.O.D. (aka Grimm Organization of Defense), but it hadn't really gotten off the ground yet as far as she could tell.

Just then, two trolls passed Snowflake carrying a stack of medium-size mirrors out the door and into the hall. Behind them came another troll carrying a single mirror that anyone could see was much too big for one troll to handle. Struggling, he bumped Ms. Jabberwocky's desk and sent a bunch of papers to the floor. When he nearly dropped the mirror, too, Ms. Jabberwocky and two princes named Awesome and Foulsmell pitched in to rescue it.

"Thanks," the troll told them, sounding relieved. "Wouldn't want to upset the big guy." He nodded toward the principal's office.

"No worries," replied Ms. Jabberwocky. "We all need a mimsy bit of help now and then." Once the troll was gone, she moved toward her desk and spoke to the gathered students. "I've called you to the office to let you know you're all being temporarily transferred out of Scrying class until we locate a new instructor."

Phew, thought Snowflake. Looked like Ms. Queenharts hadn't ratted on her about her bad quiz grade in Comportment as she'd assumed. Maybe she'd cut that teacher some slack and try to think more kindly of her from now on.

Snow White and Rose had been busily picking up the papers that had fallen. They handed them to Ms. Jabberwocky, who pulled a somewhat scorched sheet of vellum from the stack. Reading from it, she quickly began calling out reassignments.

Her eyes on the list, Ms. Jabberwocky eventually came to Snowflake's name. "Let's see, you have Scrying fourth period. You'll be reassigned to Drama. It's in the auditorium."

Snowflake wasn't sure this was such a great thing. Drama wouldn't be like most classes where you could sit at a desk and keep to yourself. No, she'd be expected to speak up in Drama and interact with other students. It would be hard to lurk and be standoffish. Not at all a good fit.

"Can I choose a different class?" she asked.

Ms. Jabberwocky frowned. "I'm sorry, but since the auditorium can easily absorb a tulgey large number of students, your entire class is being reassigned there. You'll have to make the best of it."

Stomp! Stomp! Before Snowflake could protest further, the principal came out of his office. He had a long nose and a long chin, and wore a tall hat. Although the troll had called him a "big guy," he was actually a gnome, three feet tall at most. Which was still a little taller than the trolls, though.

He came to a dead stop right in front of her. *Uh-oh*, she thought. *I'm in trouble now.* Maybe she'd been too quick to think Ms. Queenharts hadn't tattled on her.

But all the principal said, or rather *shouted*, was, "You're new? Good! Another candidate. Come with me." Snowflake winced. He might be small, but his voice was loud. Without waiting for her to answer in the affirmative, he headed back into his office, obviously expecting her to follow.

"Go on in and try," Ms. Jabberwocky urged her when she didn't move right away. "You're one of his last hopes. Every other student here at GA has tried and failed to spin the straw into gold. We were expecting that straw would be the answer to the Academy's money troubles. But after so many failures, it's looking, well, grim."

Snowflake knew all that. She'd heard kids talking. It was said that the straw could be spun into gold by the right person, if only that person could be found. She would have thought that "right person" would be Principal Rumpelstiltskin himself, since he'd done so in his fairy tale. But for some reason, that didn't seem to be the case.

"Soon, it'll be back to our alchemy experiments if we can't figure out the secret of the straw!" yelled the principal, overhearing.

"Can't say I'll be sorry," Ms. Jabberwocky merrily called back. "Those experiments were a blast, if you know what I mean. A *fiery* blast." She laughed at her own joke, snorting out a quick blast of smoke.

Warily eyeing Ms. Jabberwocky's fire-breathing snout, Snowflake darted for the principal's office. Unfortunately, the dragon lady followed, leaving the other students to wait.

"Good luck!" Snow White called after Snowflake. She touched the four-leaf-clover amulet she wore on a chain around her neck. That was nice of her. Snowflake almost thanked her, but then, in the nick of time, thought better of it and pretended not to hear.

Once inside Principal R's office, Snowflake could see that, although the troll movers had already removed a dozen or so mirrors, there were still many more on the walls to take down. Her eyes slid from the mirrors to an old wooden spinning wheel that stood in a corner. A mirror had been leaning against the wheel but now a troll headed out of the office with it. Considering she'd only replaced the principal for a very short time, Ms. Wicked had certainly left her stamp on this office. But once her mirrors were gone, the room would become Principal R's again.

Snowflake sat on the stool beside the spindle. When the principal pulled a single magic piece of straw out from under his hatband, she took a turn at trying to spin it into gold using both hands to twist the straw onto the spindle, which was really just a tall wooden spool. She wasn't surprised when she failed.

Principal R sighed, took the straw from her, and stuck it back under the band encircling the top part of his hat. Looking a bit crabby now, he silently trudged over to sit on the throne behind his desk.

As Snowflake stood, she watched Ms. Jabberwocky check her name off a long list. "I don't get it. Why doesn't

Principal R spin the gold himself?" Snowflake wondered in a quiet voice.

Looking alarmed, Ms. Jabberwocky put a long, bony green finger to her lips and shook her head to shush her.

Snowflake thought she'd spoken too softly for anyone except Ms. Jabberwocky to hear, but now she noticed through the open doorway that everyone in the outer office had gone quiet. And they weren't the only ones to have heard.

"It's not my fault!" Principal R shouted, his face turning beet red. "Don't you think I've tried to spin the straw into gold?"

To Snowflake's amazement, he proceeded to hop up on the seat of his throne and from there onto his desk. Stomping his feet, he ripped off his hat. Then he started jumping around on the desk like a crazed cricket. Her jaw dropped at the sight. Maybe Cranky-Cricketstiltskin would be a good nickname for him! Though it *was* kind of a mouthful.

A teacher at her old school had once said that anger sometimes came from embarrassment. Had her question made the principal feel embarrassed that he had failed at spinning the straw into gold? And had that embarrassment swelled into this uncontrollable anger? She knew what a grimmawful feeling that was because there were times she got really, really mad, too. Usually, with disastrous *magical* results, like the time she'd somehow conjured up a swarm of albino bees to sting some mean girls in her village. She really wished she hadn't said anything to upset him.

Ms. Jabberwocky tried to smooth things over, ushering Snowflake back into the outer office. "He'll calm down in a little while," she assured her.

"Good try with that straw," Rose said in sympathy when Snowflake rejoined the girls.

"Yeah, its magic is really turning out to be tough to crack," added Snow White.

"Brillig! All this hard work. I need a snack," Ms. Jabberwocky declared. Using two fingers, she fished up a jalapeño pepper from a jar on her desk that was sitting next to what appeared to be an oversize glass bowling ball. No, it was a big snow globe, Snowflake realized. She looked on in horror as the office assistant tilted her head back and opened her jaws wide, displaying sharp dragon teeth. With a toss of her clawed green hand, the hot pepper flew up into the air. When it fell and met her dragon fire, who knew what could happen?

Snowflake didn't want to wait around to see more. Fleeing what she assumed was imminent fire danger, she sprinted for the exit. But before she got far, a boy stepped into the office, blocking her way out. It was the boy, er, *prince* she'd met in the hall. And he was wearing a gold crown now.

"O frabjous day!" Ms. Jabberwocky had chomped the pepper in seconds flat and now rushed toward the prince. Her snout was curved into a big-toothed smile.

At the same time, the principal came out of his office. He was smiling now, too. So just as Ms. Jabberwocky had implied, his anger didn't last long. Snowflake's anger was like that, too. Quick to come, quick to go.

"Look, gimble girls and boys! This is my nephew," Ms. Jabberwocky informed the remaining students in the office. She beamed proudly at the prince.

What? thought Snowflake. But this boy didn't look anything like a dragon!

Ms. Jabberwocky's nephew grinned and whipped off his crown momentarily, favoring them with a princely bow. "The name's Dragonbreath," he said.

"*Prince* Dragonbreath," his dragon aunt added. "From the royal side of our family."

The other girls greeted him with curtsies and the boys with welcoming phrases. However, Snowflake backed away, staring at him with wide eyes. "You're a d-d-dragon?"

"Best shape-shifter in his school. First in his flame-throwing class this semester, too," bragged Ms. Jabberwocky. "Show them, Dragonbreath," she said to the prince.

"No! That's okay," said Snowflake, edging around the prince and toward the door again.

Oops! In her haste to be off, she bumped one of the trolls. She watched in dismay as the large gold-framed oval mirror he'd been carrying knocked more stuff off Ms. Jabberwocky's desk.

"Bandersnatch!" Ms. Jabberwocky shouted in alarm. "That mirror was Ms. Wicked's favorite one — the mirror she escaped through to the Nothingterror!"

After that, everything seemed to happen in slow motion. Papers fluttering everywhere. Something heavy — the snow globe! — bouncing off the mirror. The globe hitting the floor and rolling over into a corner of the room. The mirror falling to the floor.

Crash! The students all stared as the mirror broke. Its glass splintered, sending dozens of dangerously sharp shards flying outward.

"Look out!" shouted Prince Dragonbreath. He leaped in front of Snowflake and the other girls to protect them from danger.

Snowflake was mortified. This whole catastrophe was all her fault! Swift anger swelled inside her. Oh, why did this have to happen? She'd only been here a week and already . . . disaster!

Don't get upset, she tried to tell herself.

She knew that the anger she was feeling came from embarrassment, as perhaps the principal's anger had earlier. She'd caused such a mess, such trouble, in front of everyone! But although she struggled to rein in her swirling emotions, the anger escaped. She could feel her cheeks turn red. Her hands clenched into fists.

"Chill," she whispered, trying to calm herself down. But the word turned out to have a surprisingly different effect. Before her very eyes, everyone in the office froze in their tracks. *Literally!*

4
The Mirror

Snowflake backed against the office wall and stared in shock at the immobile figures all around her. Before she could decide what to do, the small shards of mirrored glass magically lifted from the floor where they'd fallen and began to swirl, forming a tornado. Within seconds, it grew larger and wilder, blowing her hair and skirt. Finally, the shard tornado turned sideways and was abruptly sucked through the office window to whirl out of sight. Weird!

But Snowflake was more concerned about everyone else in the room. They were all still frozen in various poses. Prince Dragonbreath's arms were outspread in the act of trying to protect her and the other girls from the shards. There were astonished expressions on Snow White's and Rose's pretty faces. And then there was Red Riding Hood, a girl from Snowflake's Scrying class, who had entered the office just as that icy magic had let itself loose. Red had become a statue in the act of opening the lid of a basket she held over one arm.

Snowflake shivered. Where had this new "chill" ability of hers come from, anyway? Her upset feelings had caused odd things to happen before, but this was the first time she'd actually *frozen* anyone. Oh, if only she could control her emotions!

In the middle of the office, two of the trolls were stiffly posed in comical stances, having bumped into each other as they lunged to save the mirror before more harm befell it. Beyond them stood Ms. Jabberwocky. A snort of fiery billowing smoke had hardened in a cloud shape to hang a few inches away from her snout. And the principal had frozen in angry mid-hop, hovering about a foot above the floor.

Snowflake touched the arm of the nearest girl, Rose. To her surprise, Rose's arm wasn't cold. Though everyone appeared frozen, they were quickly beginning to thaw out. *Phew!* In fact, she could already see some of them starting to move a little. Fingers twitched. Locks of hair shifted. What a relief to learn that her chilly magic was wearing off!

But what now? What would Principal R say when he unfroze? When his letter requesting her attendance at this academy had come to the orphanage last week, it had mentioned her "budding powers." How he had heard about them she had no clue. But if the rumors were true, at least part of the reason she'd been invited here was because he wanted to keep an eye on those powers. She had a feeling the principal wasn't going to approve of being turned into an icicle.

Panicking, she gazed wildly at the still-life figures around her. What should she do? Pose stiffly and pretend she'd been frozen, too, so others wouldn't guess she'd been responsible for this? No! An impulse to flee shot through her, and she dashed for the door. *Oops!* She stumbled over the mirror frame along the way and fell. As she stood and righted herself, she picked it up. Although it was four feet tall, it wasn't all that heavy with its glass gone.

She started to lean it against Ms. Jabberwocky's desk, but then behind her she heard the principal yawn as if waking up from a long sleep. Panicking anew, Snowflake ran out of the office, accidentally taking the frame with her.

Talk about a dumb move! She rushed down the hall. What was she going to do with it?

The library! She would simply take the broken mirror to the *M* section herself.

Since there had been many students in the office, it was unlikely anyone would note her disappearance when they unfroze. If she stashed the mirror fast enough, they might think another troll had taken it to the library. Anyway, they'd have no reason to assume she'd been responsible for freezing them, right? Yeah!

Lucky for her, the library hadn't moved yet. It was still just a few doors down from the office. And even luckier, its door was still propped open.

"Thank grimmness!" Snowflake muttered. At her words, the library's brass doorknob morphed into a face. A goose face with a beak. Ignoring it, she zipped past into the Grimmstone Library.

"Honk! Wait! Free entry is only for mirror-toting trolls. You, however, must answer a riddle before entering!" the gooseknob protested.

"Shh! Sorry! I'll answer two riddles next time. Promise!" she hissed over her shoulder.

The gooseknob honked at her several more times, but finally gave up. Snowflake felt kind of sorry for the knob. It had an important job to do — guarding the library's contents — and didn't get much respect for trying to do it. Probably because it was a bit annoying at times. Often *more* than a bit, actually.

Snowflake lugged the mirror frame past the *A* section and into the library aisles, which stretched so far into the distance that she could see no end to them. Row after row of shelves and little rooms were filled with who knew what.

The Grimm brothers, Wilhelm and Jacob, had built this library to protect their books and books written by many other great authors as well as various artifacts.

Although Ms. Wicked's mirror frame wasn't particularly heavy, it *was* unwieldy. Snowflake's arms and shoulders ached from carrying it already, and she was only up to Section *B*! There, she passed shelves with boxes, bats, balls, blankies, binkies, boo-boos, and bye-byes.

As she scurried along, a snow-white goose zoomed high overhead. Two more swooped in from the left, and a fourth flew in from the right. They were all going in different directions. A net dangled from each goose's bright orange beak. Some of the net bags held books. Others held random objects such as paintbrushes, lamps, or alphabet blocks that were being delivered to various sections of the library. If the geese noticed her, would they report her activities to the librarian?

Snowflake switched to dragging the mirror instead of carrying it. Which looked pretty suspicious. She'd never make it to *M*. Why hadn't she just left this frame in the office? Well, she was stuck with it now. Luckily, in Section *C*, she noticed a cart with wheels. Thank grimmness! After setting the mirror frame on it, she pulled it to *M* in no time and set it with the stack of Ms. Wicked's other mirrors.

Phew! Glad to be rid of it, she turned back and headed for Section *F*, which ended against a side wall. All along the library walls, there were whole rooms that had been lifted out of actual houses — or fabulous castles. It was amazing that all this stuff could fit in here. At times, the Grimmstone Library seemed bigger than the school itself. And no wonder! She'd heard it could magically make itself as big or as small as it chose.

Eventually, she entered Section *F*. Some of the rooms along the library wall here were decorated with furnishings such as chairs, tables, lamps, rugs, and wallpaper. One room had a sign on the door that read: A ROOM OF UPSIDE DOWN, with upside-down furniture stuck on its fluted ceiling. The Room of Mistakes had a door that had by some freaky fluke of fate been hinged in sideways.

If someone really wanted to, they could probably live in one of these rooms. And little did anyone know that Snowflake secretly did exactly that!

Still a dozen or so aisles away from the room she had appropriated as her own, she let her gaze wander to the huge chandelier and magnificently decorated ceiling above. *How did the Grimm brothers build this library to support such an enormous roof?* she wondered for the grimmzillionth time as she admired the architecture. And what kind of magical support structure allowed this place to grow bigger and smaller on a whim?

She was so busy looking up that she didn't notice Ms. Goose until it was too late to duck her.

"Snowflake!" The librarian stood before her, blocking the aisle and wearing her trademark frilly white cap and spectacles. Her crisp white apron had a curlicue *L* embroidered on its front bib. *L* for librarian, of course.

"Still researching your nursery rhyme?" Ms. Goose asked. "You are a dedicated student! Any luck finding which rhyme is yours?"

Relieved that the sharp-eyed librarian didn't seem to suspect anything was up, Snowflake shook her head. "No, there are a lot more nursery rhymes than I thought. I've been through all the ones you wrote — the Mother Goose ones. But there are tons of others besides those. It's not going to be easy."

Another part of the reason she'd been sent to this academy was to do research to find out which character she was in literature. At least that's what the grandmother back at the orphanage had told her. She hadn't said if that information was considered necessary to protect Snowflake or to protect others *from* her. Maybe no one was sure . . . yet.

Even if she didn't like what she ultimately found out about herself, she wanted to know. And this was her big chance. Everything she needed to learn her identity was likely right here somewhere on the Grimmstone Library shelves.

"Don't worry, something in this library will jump out at you one day," Ms. Goose told her as if reading her mind. "Something that *fits*. Then you'll be filled with recognition. You'll just know."

Snowflake shrugged. "Well, that hasn't happened yet. But I'll keep digging." She began sidling off, in a hurry to get away. Ms. Goose was nice, but a little too clever and a little too much in her business. There were things she didn't want this librarian to figure out. Like that Snowflake spent way more time — day *and night* — in this library than anyone realized!

Flap! Flap! At the sound of beating wings, a shadow fell over them both. They backed away to allow a winged goose as big as a horse to swoop down from above. Once it landed, the librarian hopped on its back. She and the goose lifted off the ground a few feet, but then hovered in place a moment.

"I know you're worried you might turn out to be the evil character in your tale or nursery rhyme," Ms. Goose said, surprising her. "But remember, you were sent to Grimm Academy because both good *and* evil characters from literature are welcome here. There's a place for everyone."

"Mm-hmm," Snowflake said skeptically. Everyone knew it was better to be good than evil. Ms. Goose was just trying to make her feel better.

Most of the time she felt totally normal. But she could tell that her powers were growing stronger. It scared her that she didn't know how to control them or even what those powers were exactly. What if she never found out who she was and why she had these powers? What if everything just got worse and worse and worse? What if, instead of summoning albino bees and freezing people into temporary statues whenever she got upset, she discovered she had the power to call forth Dastardlies from the Dark Nothingterror or something really awful like that? How would this librarian — or any of the others at GA — like her then?

"Well, keep trying. And let me know if you need help finding anything. My filing system can be a trifle loosey-goosey at times," Ms. Goose told her with a quick wink.

"Okay."

Flap! Flap! Within seconds, Ms. Goose was airborne and flying across the library.

Once she was gone, Snowflake darted farther into Section *F*. Finally, after looking right and left to make sure no one was watching, she turned a doorknob and scooted into her room. The one she had chosen as her temporary bedroom, anyway. She more or less camped out in here after school and all night. No one knew about her hideaway, not even Mary Mary Quite Contrary, the roommate she'd been originally assigned to (but bailed on).

A tall stack of nursery rhyme books she had borrowed from the library sat on a footstool in her room. She grabbed one of them and climbed atop the pile of feather-filled mattresses set on a sturdy futon that served as her bed. At night, she usually tucked herself between the two mattresses at the top with only her head sticking out so that she could scooch down to hide if Ms. Goose came around unexpectedly. Once or twice she'd had to stifle a sneeze caused by an escaped feather in order not to get caught.

Luckily there was an *F* for *fountain* in her room. It bubbled merrily and helped disguise any noise she made. Plus it came in handy as a shower. She'd hung the few gowns she'd brought from the orphanage on hangers she'd scored from Section *H* along a pole she'd gotten from Section *P*. Plus she'd rounded up other things she needed, like soap and towels from the *S* and *T* sections of the library. Food was easy to come by. She was in the *F* section after all!

37

Lying on her bed now, she opened the book of nursery rhymes she'd selected and skimmed through it, looking for a hint of anything that *fit*, as Ms. Goose suggested. She wasn't expecting to find any such thing, but suddenly, she sat up straight, stunned.

Under the simple title of "There Was a Little Girl," authored by some guy named Henry Wadsworth Longfellow, she read this rhyme:

There was a little girl
Who had a little curl
Right in the middle of her forehead;
And when she was good
She was very, very good,
But when she was bad she was horrid.

Could this be her nursery rhyme? Was *she* horrid? Snowflake wondered. Those girls in her village who'd been stung by the albino bees she'd magicked up that day would probably say so. *Sigh.* She didn't have a curl in the middle of her forehead, though. She had longish bangs that some-times got wavy, especially in damp weather. Sadly, this was the closest *F* for fit so far, though. She bookmarked the page, then scrambled down to set the book in a far cor-ner of the floor in her stack of *F*-for-*feasible* books (which meant those containing rhymes that might possibly turn out to be hers).

The only other nursery rhymes in her stack so far were there simply because they contained half of her name in them. Like this one Ms. Goose herself had penned:

Mary had a little lamb,
little lamb,
little lamb.
Mary had a little lamb,
Its fleece was white as snow.

Okay. Maybe the connection was slight. She didn't have a lamb or anything. She would keep looking for other nursery rhymes. And in the meantime, she'd wait to show anyone the *horrid* one till she'd considered it some more.

5

Jack Frost

$\mathcal{M}$eanwhile, back in the principal's office . . .

Still trapped inside his glass globe, Jack Frost zipped over and nabbed the broom the fake snowman was holding. Then he rushed back to poke the tip end of the broom's handle into the crack that had formed when the globe had gotten knocked onto the floor. He had just begun to work the handle like a crowbar to widen the crack when he heard someone shout, "Look out!"

Huh? He paused. He couldn't see anything — his globe had rolled into a dark corner. But during the next few seconds, he became aware that an eerie silence had settled over the office. Sounds were muffled inside his globe, but he could usually make out the dull roar of voices and people moving around. For several minutes, as he went back to widening the crack in his globe with his makeshift crowbar, there was none of that.

Then, suddenly, a weird, whirling noise that sounded for all the world like a wild windstorm started up. It only lasted a few moments. Gradually the muffled sounds of voices and movement began again.

Strange, thought Jack. What was going on out there? He shook his head to clear it, causing the two tassels on his knit cap to whack the tiny snowflakes inside the globe and send them flying. Then he went back to work, and the fracture started to widen.

Crrack! Jack pushed through. In seconds, he was out of the snow globe. He was free! He zoomed upward, doing quadruple somersaults in the air and flitting joyfully around the office.

"How did that bat get in here?" yelled Principal R, pointing up at him.

The dragon lady squinted at Jack. "That's not a bat. I think it's an uffish brownie!" she shouted.

"Or maybe a pixie," suggested a tall boy wearing a crown.

"Or a leprechaun," added a girl wearing a four-leaf-clover necklace.

"You're all wrong!" Jack Frost exclaimed huffily. "I'm a sprite! The Grimm brothers trapped me in that snow globe over there on the floor, and I just now escaped." He grinned gleefully at the principal. "So what do you think of that, Rumpelstiltskin?"

Frosted faux pas! It had not been a good idea to rile the GA principal by speaking his actual name. Especially since Jack had overheard students say that doing so was against school rules. Too late to call back his boo-boo, though.

The principal had already begun to hop around and shake his fists angrily. The single straw poking up from his hatband fell to the ground, and he picked it up. Jack couldn't help noticing that the straw gleamed as bright as gold in the principal's grasp. Without much to do within the limited range of his snow globe, Jack's senses had become very finely tuned, and there wasn't much he *didn't* notice!

The boy in the crown went over and picked up the cracked snow globe. He handed it to Ms. Jabberwocky. "Looks like that sprite is telling the truth."

"Bandersnatch! He broke out of this, you mean?" she said, studying the globe. "I whiffled this thing out of the library only this morning to use as a paperweight."

"You what?" yelled the principal. "The brothers Grimm must've trapped him in there for a reason. Quick! He has to go back inside it. Get him, Ms. J!"

Following orders, Ms. Jabberwocky whipped out the tip of her tail. *Whack!* Taken by surprise, Jack Frost found himself lassoed. As her tail held him captive, the others in the office discussed how best to stick him back in the snow globe and repair its crack.

No! He wouldn't let himself be imprisoned again. He wanted to be free! Plus, he needed time to find an evil substitute for Ms. Wicked. Someone with magic more powerful than his who could help him achieve his destiny. Quickly, he made something up to convince everyone to release him.

"Did you ever think that maybe the Grimm brothers put me in that snow globe so Ms. Jabberwocky would find me on the very day you needed me most?" he demanded.

"Why would we need you?" scoffed the principal. Having quickly calmed down, he stuck the piece of straw back into his hatband. Now when he held it, it didn't gleam gold, however. It had only gleamed in the principal's hand when he had gotten furious. Interesting. Putting two and two together, Jack got an idea.

"You *need* me because I can spin that straw of yours into gold," he claimed quickly. "I can't reach the spindle, though, so you'll have to do the spinning while I sit on your shoulder giving directions."

Although no one seemed to buy this at first, Jack Frost persisted until he persuaded them to give it a try. Once Principal R was at the spindle, Jack perched on his shoulder and intentionally called him "Rumpelstiltskin."

The inevitable temper fit occurred. And, lo and behold, the straw gleamed more brightly again. Plus, it lengthened endlessly in the principal's hands, as he was suddenly able to spin it into a pile of gold! Principal R, the dragon lady, and the students gathered around to stare in amazement at the heap of spun gold they thought Jack Frost had created.

"Callooh! Callay! This will bring the realm frabjous wealth!" shouted Ms. Jabberwocky.

"Wait a minute," said Principal R. He frowned with suspicion, then brushed Jack off his shoulder. Again, the principal tried to spin the straw into gold, but all by himself this time. However, he was calm now, so he couldn't do it.

The principal stood and spoke to Jack. "Okay, I'm convinced. *You* spun the straw into gold. As a reward, you may go free. But only if you agree to spin more gold for us whenever we need it."

Jack Frost quickly agreed to do so, as long as the principal continued to help. And he made an additional bargain. "Allow me to search the Academy for a talented teacher or student with special skills. Someone I can train to spin the straw, too!"

The principal nodded. Running GA took a lot of time after all. It would save him some work if others could help Jack spin. A deal was struck.

Little did Principal Rumpelstiltskin know that he was the *only* one who could spin the straw into gold. And that he could do it *without* a sprite sitting on his shoulder. It was his temper that somehow gave the principal the power to spin gold. But only Jack Frost held that secret, and he wasn't about to tell anyone. He hoped his ploy would allow him time enough to find a truly, frostastically wicked teacher or student to boss around, er, become a sidekick for.

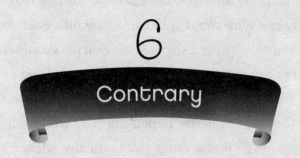

6

Contrary

When Snowflake woke the next morning, she fetched some fruit and French toast for breakfast from the *F*-for-*food* shelf right outside her room in the library. Most students ate in the Great Hall, but not her. It would be unwise to do so, since that could lead to chatting with others, which could lead to making friends. Not that she didn't ever get lonely, mind you. She did. But this was just the way things had to be.

After breakfast, she headed out to first-period Sieges, Catapults, and Jousts class on the lawn outside Gray Castle. Before she could reach the river and take a boat across to that side of the Academy, however, she heard a voice over in the Bouquet Garden yell, "Ow! Ow!" And then, "Stop! Stop! Come out of there!"

Thinking someone was hurt, Snowflake ran over. In the garden, she found Mary Mary Quite Contrary hunched over her flower bushes, apparently talking to them. Mary Mary, of course, was supposed to have been Snowflake's roommate.

"What's wrong?" Snowflake asked her.

"Something pricked me," said Mary Mary.

"Like a thorn?"

"Yeah, I guess, I guess. Sort of like that," said Mary Mary. She had a tendency to repeat words and phrases, Snowflake had noticed. Sort of like her name was a repeat.

"Where's the thorn? Want me to help get it out?" Snowflake asked. She stepped closer to Mary Mary and looked at the place on her arm she was rubbing. She didn't see any blood there, only a fading reddish mark.

"It's fine now," the girl said. "It doesn't hurt anymore."

"Oh, good. Must not have been that bad of a prick after all," Snowflake commented. She glanced around. "Who were you talking to in the bushes a minute ago?"

As if she hadn't heard Snowflake's question, Mary Mary abruptly dived into a clump of chrysanthemums. "Stop that! Stop that!" Mary Mary cried. She was yelling at the flowers!

It wasn't unusual for Mary Mary to be quite contrary (as the name of her nursery rhyme suggested) with GA students. But she had always acted kind and loving toward these flowers she grew anytime Snowflake had passed by her in her garden. So why was she so mad at them?

47

"Shush!" the contrary girl suddenly ordered Snowflake.

Huh? Was Mary Mary mad at her now, too? Maybe that shouldn't have come as such a surprise, knowing her contrary nature. In fact, this girl seemed to have taken a special dislike to Snowflake from day one. Or so Snowflake had thought when Mary Mary had acted so annoyed about everything the morning they'd met in Emerald Tower and learned they were to share a dorm room. That was why she had told this garden girl she'd make other arrangements. And on her own, she'd promptly found a room for herself in the library.

Mary Mary was glad she wasn't rooming with her, Snowflake was almost certain. But she hoped this girl wouldn't ask where she had ended up staying because Snowflake didn't want anyone to know she was sleeping in the library.

Just then, both girls heard a rustling in the bushes nearby. "Aha! There he is. Come out, come out, you naughty, naughty nibbler!" yelled Mary Mary.

Nibbler? Who in the world was she talking to?

"You guard this area, and I'll go over there and flush him out," Mary Mary instructed, pointing to the rustling bushes.

"Flush who out?" asked Snowflake. Reluctantly, she did

as asked even though Mary Mary was too intent on her objective to explain.

While waiting to see what would happen, Snowflake admired and sniffed the flowers surrounding her. An extraordinary variety of them grew here in the Bouquet Garden — roses, tulips, lilies, daisies, carnations, orchids, and dozens more. Unlike most flowers, though, these actually bloomed together in attractive combinations. Every bush grew numerous ready-made bouquets that contained many types of flowers. So with a single flick of your wrist, you could pick a beautifully arranged bouquet anytime you wanted.

Caring for this garden was Mary Mary's special task. All the students at GA were assigned a "tower task" at the start of their year. However, Snowflake hadn't been given hers yet.

What was Mary Mary doing over there? Snowflake needed to get to class. "I really have to —" she started to say, easing away.

"Aha! Gotcha, you little chrysanthemum muncher." Mary Mary reached into the mums and pulled out . . . a white bunny! A mischievous-looking one that had been eating her garden, apparently. He wriggled out of her grasp and bounded across the clearing toward Snowflake.

"Quick, get him!" shouted Mary Mary. For some reason, her eyes appeared strangely glazed. Or was that just a trick of the sunlight?

Before Snowflake could make a move toward the pesky bunny as instructed, he leaped right into her arms! He twitched his ears and wiggled his nose at her as if saying hello. "Hi, cutie pie," she murmured to him. A second later, he leaped away again and escaped back into the bushes.

"Leaping lagomorphs!" muttered Mary Mary. With a sigh of annoyance, she gave up on the bunny for the moment and went back to tending her flowers. While she was bent over her hydrangeas, Snowflake snuck off to class.

First-period Sieges, Catapults, and Jousts was just getting started when she finally arrived. Coach Candlestick had instructed them to practice lobbing hay bales with catapults all week. A few days ago, Snowflake's had made it all the way from shore to land on Maze Island in the middle of the river.

Normally, this class moved indoors on Fridays. But today, they would remain outside. Some students would shift to catapulting items other than hay bales, while others would switch to new skills.

As they loaded, aimed, and fired various objects from the catapult, everyone was abuzz about an announcement

Principal R had made at breakfast. Apparently, sometime after Snowflake had left the office to return the mirror frame to the library, a sprite named Jack Frost had appeared to spin the principal's magical straw into gold. And now this sprite planned to select someone at GA that he would train in the art of gold spinning to assist him in making more.

"Any pumpkins left?" asked a student named Goldilocks, who was next up at the catapult.

Snowflake and the others hunted around and came up with one. As it was passed to Goldilocks, Snowflake reflected that she'd never met a sprite and didn't really know what one looked like. She listened carefully, but her classmates hadn't been introduced to this Jack Frost and didn't seem to know anything about him.

Still, his arrival was mildly interesting news. But the really *good* news was that no one was talking about her putting a big chill on everyone in the office yesterday! Distracted by the sprite, they must not have taken time to wonder what had happened to them or to the missing mirror frame, she decided in relief. Or maybe they had no memory of being frozen at all.

Boing! Everyone cheered as Goldilocks catapulted her pumpkin in a high arc to land in the river with a *plop!* After recording her distance on her student log, she remarked, "I wonder how that sprite is going to choose who is most trainable?"

"I heard he's giving tests," replied Rapunzel, the Grimm girl who'd found the magic straw in the first place.

"Tests?" Snowflake's ears perked up, and not in a happy way. She listened closely, wanting information that might help her avoid this test. After all, hadn't she been tested in Principal R's office only yesterday? She'd already shown she couldn't spin straw into gold.

As if he'd read her mind, Prince Foulsmell (who actually wasn't at all stinky, thank goodness), said, "But Principal R already tested everyone. None of us could change that straw into gold."

Rapunzel shrugged. "I guess Jack Frost thinks his test will somehow find people that Principal R's trials didn't discover."

They began making funny guesses about what the sprite's test would be like. "Maybe we'll have to balance the straw on the tip of our noses and walk around the spindle three times," suggested Foulsmell.

"Or maybe Jack Frost will want to see who can flick that magic straw the farthest," said Goldilocks.

"Or he could drop it in one of our hay bales, and who-ever finds it aces the test!" said Rapunzel. Soon, everyone was laughing, including Snowflake.

"Snowflake!" Uh-oh. Coach Candlestick had noticed her laughing and goofing around and was waving her over. When she was at his side, he looked at a list on his clipboard and said, "Let's see, you've been on the catapult all week, right? Let's try something new. Are you up for masketball?"

Snowflake wrinkled her nose and shook her head. That was a game where you wore masks and shot balls at hoops that moved around. She liked watching the game, but not playing it.

"Okay. How about candlestick jumping?" he queried hopefully. That skill was part of his nursery rhyme, she knew, and he had a team of students that competed in the sport.

"Jump over an open flame?" She shook her head harder. Definitely no.

"Jousting? Swordplay? You can't do catapulting all semester," he informed her.

Just then, Snowflake had an idea. "Who builds them? The catapults, I mean. Could I design a new one here in class?"

The coach punched a cheerful fist in the air. "Sure! I like the enthusiasm!" He looked down at his ledger and wrote two words by her name: *catapult testing*.

She frowned. Testing? Well, she supposed testing was part of building a catapult, so whatever.

She hadn't really studied how the catapults worked before, but now she did. After a while, Rapunzel wandered over to ask what she was doing, and Snowflake explained.

"Need any help?" Rapunzel asked eagerly.

"That's okay," Snowflake replied, shaking her head. She didn't notice when Rapunzel shot her a look of disappointment. Because Snowflake's mind was preoccupied, and not only with catapults. For some weird reason, she couldn't stop thinking about that cute bunny.

All during the rest of her morning classes, she kept wondering if he would be all right on his own. She was so concerned for his welfare, in fact, that she stopped by the Bouquet Garden before lunch just to check on him.

7
Cuddly Cuteness

$\mathcal{L}$uckily, Mary Mary was nowhere in sight when Snowflake returned to the Bouquet Garden. Neither was anyone else.

"Here, bunny, bunny," she called softly, while peeking under bushes. "You okay in there?"

A pale pink nose poked out of some leaves. Then whiskers followed. And a mischievous face. Then the whole bunny hopped out. Snowflake sat down cross-legged in the grass, and the bunny jumped into her lap. She cuddled him. His snow-white fur was like velvet. When she tried to pet his ears, though, he twitched them away. "Okay, got it. You don't like having your ears touched."

In seconds, the bunny was asleep in her lap. Snowflake had always had a soft spot for animals. She used to pet all the cats, dogs, cows, and even chickens in her village when she'd walked to and from school. And this bunny was adorable.

Suddenly, she heard footsteps. Mary Mary was coming! Snowflake gently pushed the bunny off of her lap and shooed him back into the flower bushes again. "Quick! Hide."

The bunny obeyed, scampering away in the nick of time.

Mary Mary made a sour face when she saw Snowflake rising from the grass. Or maybe that was her pleased expression. It was hard to tell the difference sometimes with this contrary girl.

"Oh, it's you," Mary Mary said. "I thought I caught a glimpse of that bunny a second ago. Did you see him, too?" she asked, poking around in the bushes.

"Um, no, I . . ." Snowflake began. She wasn't going to get that cutie patootie bunny in trouble! But then . . . *Boing!* The bunny leaped from the bushes and into her arms. As Mary Mary frowned at her, probably suspecting she hadn't been telling the truth, Snowflake set the critter down and backed away. "Um, well, I guess I'll be heading off to lunch now."

She walked off through the garden. The bunny followed her. "You'll go back to your hideout if you know what's good for you, mister fuzzy ears," she scolded him.

Mary Mary hurried over and scooped the bunny up. She held the flower-chomping rascal out to Snowflake and said, "Here, take him. I don't want him anywhere near my garden."

"What? No!" Snowflake backed away, shaking her head. "I can't."

She didn't dare get her heart involved with this bunny, much as she might like to. In just the few seconds she'd held that long-eared furry bundle of mischief, she'd been drawn to him. Wanted to cuddle and play with him. But how could she take care of a bunny when she had no idea what her future held? What if her powers got her kicked out of GA the same way they'd gotten her booted out of her village?

She didn't even have a real, permanent room to keep this bunny in right now. Plus, she knew nothing about caring for rabbits. Back in the orphanage, they'd never been allowed any kind of pet. No! She shook her head again, turning to go.

"If you don't take him, I'll give him to the hunters in the forest," singsonged Mary Mary.

Snowflake froze in her tracks, then whipped around to stare at the girl. *Whoa!* That was a super-mean thing to say, even for Mary Mary. What was up with this girl? Did she really hate bunnies that much? She gazed into Mary Mary's eyes, puzzling anew over the odd glazed look that had come into them that morning and still remained.

"Cute bunny!" said a new voice. It was a Grimm girl with long blond hair, wearing a pink dress and glittery glass slippers. "You're Snowflake, right?" she said as she came into the garden. "I'm Cinderella, Cinda for short."

Snowflake nodded in response. She'd already figured out the girl's identity and fairy tale. Those glass slippers were a dead giveaway.

Cinda reached out to pet the bunny Mary Mary still held. He wiggled his ears cutely. "Is he yours?" she asked Mary Mary.

"No." Mary Mary looked at Snowflake then, waiting for her to say something. When she didn't speak up immediately, Mary Mary turned away with the bunny. In the direction of the woods!

Snowflake gasped. Was that contrary girl really going to carry out her threat to deliver the bunny to some hunters? "Okay, I'll take him," Snowflake offered quickly. Whereupon Mary Mary stepped over to her and plopped the bunny in her arms.

Fritzwibbles! What was she going to do with a bunny? Snowflake thought. She was sure she'd just made a huge mistake.

"You guys can head out of my garden anytime now," Mary Mary prompted in irritation, her glazed eyes moving between Snowflake and Cinda. "I've got stuff to do here before lunch. You're keeping me from doing it." To their surprise, she smacked a ladybug off a leaf. Surely a horticulturalist like her knew they were good for gardens? The red, spotted little bugs ate sap-sucking aphids.

Cinda grinned at Snowflake and rolled her pretty blue eyes. "Somebody's in a bad mood," she murmured, but quietly so Mary Mary wouldn't hear.

"Yeah, a really bad mood," agreed Snowflake. Taking the hint, though, she and Cinda headed out of the garden together and across the lawn toward the entrance to Pink Castle.

"You're new, right?" Cinda asked her.

"Um . . . yeah," Snowflake replied. At the same time, she glanced distractedly over her shoulder at Mary Mary. She wondered if Cinda had noticed Mary Mary's glazed expression and thought the girl was acting weird, too. But before she could ask, Cinda spoke again.

"So that bunny is yours?"

Snowflake looked down at the bundle of fuzzy cuteness snuggled in her arms. Suddenly, she thought of a way to fix her pet problem before she got too attached. "Not exactly," she told Cinda. "I'm trying to find a good home for him. Would you like a pet by any chance?"

By now, the girls had reached the Pink Castle drawbridge and started across it. "Me? Thanks, but I can't take him. Honestly, my glass slippers are enough like pets for me. I have to clean them, polish them, and take them out for walks regularly or they get stir-crazy." Just then, the slippers she was wearing executed a little dance step, whirling her around. She let out a beautiful trilling laugh. "They have minds of their own sometimes!"

Cinda's glass slippers were her magic charm. Which meant they had special powers. Snowflake had heard that the slippers fit only her and could lead her to locate things she was searching for. Charms only worked for one particular person — the person they were intended for. Not every GA student had a charm, though. It could take years before you found your own special one, or it found you.

"Well, do you know anyone who might want this bunny?" Snowflake asked as he wiggled his whiskers and nuzzled her neck. *Aww. What a sweetie!*

"Hmm." Cinda cocked her head as they entered the school. "Not really. Why don't you ask around at lunch?"

Although Snowflake had always avoided hanging out with other students, this suggestion made sense. Maybe she would find someone willing to take this little guy off her hands. She couldn't keep him hidden for long in the library. And she couldn't let him loose in the garden again. Mary Mary might just carry out her threat to give him to hunters.

"Good idea," she told Cinda.

The two girls made their way to the majestic Great Hall at the center of the Academy. It was where the principal made announcements, meals were served, and fancy balls (as well as the occasional class) were held.

When they entered the Hall, some girls waved Cinda over to their table. "I'm going to say hi to my friends. Catch up with you in line in a sec, okay?" she told Snowflake.

"Sure." Even in her hurry to unload the bunny on someone else, Snowflake took time to admire the architecture of the Hall as she walked onward. This was the first time she'd been in here, since she normally ate alone, foraging for food in the library. Fascinated, she studied her surroundings now while she had the chance.

Two stories high, the Great Hall was also long and wide. Through the double rows of large arched windows on both sides of the Hall, she could see blue skies with fluffy white clouds. Birds flew in and out of the windows, sometimes swooping low to peck food crumbs from the stone floors.

Snowflake soon turned her attention to the students around her. Many were already seated at the two long tables on opposite sides of the room. Covered with white linen tablecloths, the tables stretched from one end of the enormous Hall to the other. What was the best way of finding a worthy prospective student who would give the bunny a good home? Walking up and asking kids she'd never met if they wanted a pet might be a little awkward.

While she was pondering what to do, she spotted a bunch of students holding silver trays up ahead in the lunch line. Prince Dragonbreath was there with a group of guys. It sure hadn't taken him long to make friends. She headed for the line, hoping to convince someone there to take care of the bunny snuggled in her arms.

"So which fairy tale are you from, Dragonbreath?" she heard Foulsmell ask as she came up behind the boys. Since there were so many boys whose first name was Prince around the Academy, most just went by their last names.

"Haven't been assigned to one yet," Dragonbreath replied.

"*Assigned*?" repeated a boy named Prince Prince. "You mean you don't already have a fairy tale?"

Snowflake had been wondering the same thing. Was this dragon boy tale-less like her?

"That's right. You might not have noticed, but most of the time we dragons aren't named in literature," explained Dragonbreath. "That's because there aren't enough dragons to go around. Which means we get assigned on an as-needed basis and usually wind up in more than one tale or rhyme."

Interesting, thought Snowflake, as the line crowded

forward a few steps. Was it possible she could be from more than one rhyme or fairy tale, too? Somehow she doubted it, but it was something to consider.

"Yeah, in dragon stories it's always the same. The dragon gobbles people and locks up a princess, and then some heroic prince like me comes along and saves her," said another boy wearing a crown. Prince Perfect was his name.

A frown flitted across Prince Dragonbreath's face, as if he were bothered by what Perfect had said. But he quickly hid his feelings and acted all casual.

"And guess what happens to the dragon in the end?" Perfect went on. Laughing, he drew a finger across his throat.

Well, that wasn't very nice, thought Snowflake. The way Prince Perfect was acting, he fit that "horrid" rhyme better than she did. Even if he wasn't a girl and didn't have a little curl in the middle of his forehead!

She opened her mouth to say something in Dragonbreath's defense, but Foulsmell beat her to it. "Hey, I say it's up to Dragonbreath to decide if he'll be a good or bad dragon in any given situation."

"Right you are," agreed Dragonbreath. Spotting Snowflake, he smiled. If he'd noticed her disappearance from the office yesterday, he didn't ask about it. Instead, his green eyes went to the bunny she held. "Cute. Is he yours?"

"Um, no. That is, I found him, but I'm not going to keep him." She was about to add that she was trying to find someone who would take the bunny as a pet, but she stopped herself. Because what if Dragonbreath said *he* wanted the bunny? She couldn't give him to a *dragon*. Dragonbreath might accidentally sneeze someday and fry the poor bunnykins!

"So what will you do with him, then?" Dragonbreath asked.

"I'm not sure. I . . . um . . ." As Snowflake shifted from one slippered foot to the other, Cinda came over.

"Having any luck?" asked Cinda. She smiled at the group of boys. "She's trying to give away a bunny. Any of you guys up for a new pet?"

Snowflake sent Prince Dragonbreath a guilty glance from under her eyelashes. He looked back at her with a blank expression. Kind of like how she tried to make her face look whenever she felt unsure of herself or hurt. She figured he'd guessed why she hadn't offered him the bunny. Oh, grimmrats! She'd hurt his feelings.

"Dragons and bunnies don't really mix," he said shortly. Then he turned away to order his lunch.

Foulsmell gave the bunny a pat and seemed to consider the idea. But he said, "Much as I'd like to, I'm going to have to say no. I just don't have time for a pet with homework and all." Others seemed at least mildly interested, too, but ultimately they all said no.

Eventually, the line moved ahead, and Snowflake heard a scary voice speaking to her. "Care for a fresh-baked gingerbread cookie, dearie?" it demanded. A wrinkled old hand shot into her line of vision, its fingers holding out a small plate to her. There was a three-dimensional cookie shaped like a gingerbread house on it. It looked like it would fit perfectly in Snowflake's palm and was beautifully decorated with candies and icing. Yum!

Snowflake looked up from the plate and into the eyes of the woman who'd spoken. *Whoa!* They were as yellow as a cat's! And her white-gray hair was as wild and scraggly as the moss that grew in Neverwood Forest.

At the scared look on her face, Mistress Hagscorch cackled. Did it please her to frighten the wits out of a new student? Snowflake wondered. The witchy-looking cook leaned closer and pinched her cheek, then held the plate out to her again. "Eat. We need to fatten you up!" She cackled again.

Finally noticing the bunny, Mistress Hagscorch frowned. "No bunnies allowed in the cafeteria," she pronounced. Then her expression turned hopeful. "Unless it's for a stew?"

"No!" said Snowflake, rearing back. At her abrupt move,

the surprised bunny leaped from her arms and took off through the Great Hall.

Snowflake ran after it. Why, she wasn't sure. The bunny wasn't really her problem. But she didn't want Hagscorch to turn him into stew any more than she wanted hunters to have him!

8
Lunch

Boing! Boing! Boing! Snowflake raced after the bunny as he hopped down the length of the Hall, zigzagging between the two tables. Drawing everyone's attention, he dashed around students' feet, knocking over schoolbags and anything else they'd set on the floor. She chased that bunny all the way to where the group of Cinda's friends were sitting. There, the critter leaped into an empty spot on the bench seat between Rapunzel and Red Riding Hood.

Snowflake came to a halt and glared down at him. The long-eared bunny grinned mischievously up at her. Twitching his ears and nose, he nuzzled her hand as if asking her forgiveness for having run off.

"Oh, how cute!" cooed Rapunzel.

Snowflake glanced worriedly over her shoulder. "Hagscorch is coming!" she cautioned them. "We can't let her see him. She wants to turn him into stew!"

Alarmed now, the girls at the table all leaned out from their benches to look for the cook. She was indeed running toward them. And she was waving an empty stew pot around in one hand and its matching lid in the other.

"Quick! Put him in my basket," suggested Red Riding Hood. While Snowflake and some of the other girls blocked Hagscorch's view, Red opened her nut-brown basket. About the size of a large shoe box, it had a swirly design on either end and a lid that hinged in the middle. It was her magic charm, Snowflake knew. Just like the glass slippers were Cinda's. But precisely what powers Red's basket had, she wasn't sure.

Boing! The bunny hopped in all on his own. After shutting the lid, Red slid the basket onto her lap. Then she drew the sides of her bright red cape tightly over her lap to hide the basket. Just in time!

Mistress Hagscorch screeched to a halt at their table, looking around in suspicion. "Where's that bunny?"

"Maybe it hopped out the window?" Snow White suggested innocently.

The cook looked up at the high windows and gave a snort. "I don't think so! Bunnies can't fly." She moved closer.

Rapunzel patted the empty spot on the bench between her and Red Riding Hood where the bunny had been only seconds ago. Snowflake took the hint and sat down.

"Maybe it was a magic bunny, and it simply vanished into thin air. Like the kind magicians use," Cinda suggested as she walked up and took a seat opposite Snowflake. Cinda's tray was loaded with food, including veggies like celery, romaine lettuce, and carrots. Stuff a bunny would enjoy nibbling, Snowflake realized. How thoughtful!

"Humpf!" Mistress Hagscorch obviously wasn't buying Cinda's idea as to the bunny's whereabouts, either. She looked on the floor under the table and all around, but finally gave up. "Well, if I see one hair of that hare in this Hall again, it's toast! Or stew, anyway."

After she was gone, the girls all breathed a sigh of relief. Red opened her cape again and lifted the basket lid. The bunny stared out at the girls and wiggled his nose adorably.

"I'll keep him in my basket for you till after lunch, okay?" Red Riding Hood offered.

"Sure. He seems comfy in there," Snowflake replied.

"Yeah, and we can sneak him the snacks Cinda brought now that Mistress Hagscorch is gone," added Snow White.

Cinda nodded, then gave Snowflake a small towel. After both girls quickly cleansed their hands, Cinda told her, "I got us a couple of International Meetball Hoagies to eat. Hope that's okay." She lifted a plate off her tray and passed it across the table.

"Smells grimmyummy," said Snowflake, taking the plate. Suddenly hungry, she picked up her hoagie in both hands and opened her mouth wide.

"Bonjour, il me fait plaisir d'être votre hoagie aujourd'hui. Bon appétit," said a small voice. Startled, Snowflake nearly dropped the sandwich.

"It was your hoagie," Goldilocks informed her.

"Tell it *merci*," instructed Cinda. She said it like this: mehr-*SEE*.

Sandwiches that talked? Snowflake searched the faces of the girls around her, trying to tell if they were playing a trick. But they looked sincere. "Uh, *merci*," she repeated.

"The hoagies say hello in different languages. They're the M-E-E-T-ball kind, get it?" Rapunzel explained.

"Yours is on French bread," Snow White told Snowflake. "It said, 'Hello, it's my pleasure to be your hoagie today.' And you answered, 'Thanks'."

"Mine's on Italian." Cinda picked it up and took a bite.

Instantly, a new small voice said, *"Ciao, sono un pranzo magnifico!"*

"That means, 'Hello, I am a wonderful lunch!' in Italian," Goldilocks explained, since Cinda's mouth was full now.

While they chatted, the Grimm girls began slipping veggie tidbits from Cinda's tray into Red's basket for the

70

bunny. "He's so adorable," Rapunzel said as she fed him a bit of lettuce. "How long have you had him?"

"And what's his name?" Snow White added.

"I just call him Bunny. He's not exactly mine," Snowflake explained between bites of hoagie. "I found him in Mary Mary Quite Contrary's garden chomping on her flowers. She was shooing him away. He really needs a good home." She gazed hopefully at Red Riding Hood, Snow White, Goldilocks, and then Rapunzel.

Rapunzel shook her head and the ends of her super-fast-growing, long blue-streaked black hair nearly brushed the floor. "He's sweet, but my five cats might not get along with him."

"Oh."

"And I've got a pet fur allergy," said Snow White.

"Sorry, but I only keep stuffed *toy* animals," said Goldilocks. "I do hope you find a good home for him, though."

Snowflake looked at Red Riding Hood, pinning her hopes on the red-caped girl.

"He is grimmadorable. But I just don't know . . ." Red's voice trailed off, and she looked over at the boy on her other side.

Snowflake recognized the boy as Wolfgang, the shape-shifting wolf from Red Riding Hood's fairy tale. She'd heard that he and Red hung out together a lot. What if someday Wolfgang shifted into wolf form and got hungry when the bunny was around? No, Snowflake thought with a shudder. Looked like Red was out as a bunny owner, too.

She reached into Red Riding Hood's basket and patted the bunny. His tummy full, he was almost purring. Absently, she stroked him till he curled up to nap.

As the bunny dozed off, the grandfather clock on the balcony at one end of the Hall whirred to life and said a rhyme:

"Hickory Dickory Dock,
The mouse ran up the clock.
It's now gone noon.
So classes start soon.
Hickory Dickory Dock."

On cue, the bluebirds that had been flying in and out of the Hall dipped down to the tables. They began picking up trays in their beaks and carrying them off to the kitchen. Within seconds, they returned carrying small silver bowls of warm water and new white linen hand towels, which they set before each student.

When the rhyme ended, a mechanical mouse popped out of a little door above the clock's face (which had eyes, a nose, and a mouth). The mouse squeaked twelve times to signal noon. Each squeak was followed by a low-toned bong that echoed throughout the Academy.

Time for class. Snowflake wiped her hands on her fresh towel and hopped up, anxious to get going. Because without realizing it, she had broken (or at least *bent*) her number one rule for herself: *Don't make friends!* Luckily, the girls had been too focused on the bunny to ask personal questions — such as the title of her nursery rhyme or tale. She had to admit, though, now that she had started to get to know some GA students, they were pretty nice!

It was all Mary Mary's fault. By sticking her with this bunny, she'd caused Snowflake to let down her guard. She had to find a good pet caretaker ASAP and get back to keeping to herself.

But currently, she was short on choices. "Want to keep the bunny for a while?" she asked Red Riding Hood again as the girls all got up from the table and started out of the Hall together. Red could probably be trusted to keep it away from Wolfgang, right? At least Snowflake hoped so.

Red opened her basket. They could both see that the bunny was still curled up and sleeping. "I do hate to wake him up. What do you have fourth period?" she asked Snowflake. "Oh, wait, you were in Scrying with me. I'm so glad our class got moved to Drama now. I'm in love with acting!"

"And she's the best actor at school," added Rapunzel, who was walking right behind them.

Snowflake knew that, of course. In the library, she'd seen a poster from a play Red and Wolfgang had starred in earlier in the year called *Red Robin Hood*. "But don't you already have Drama *third* period?" she asked Red.

Red Riding Hood looked at her in surprise. Probably thought she was some kind of spy or something for knowing that. Thing was, when you didn't have friends, you had lots of time to observe others around you. And every day when Snowflake headed for Calligraphy and Illuminated Manuscripts class third period, she'd seen Red heading for Drama in the auditorium.

"I do," Red replied. "But ever since Scrying got canceled, I've been begging Ms. Jabberwocky to let me take Drama third *and* fourth. Yesterday, she finally caved. At least, until we get another Scrying teacher."

As they left the Hall, Red Riding Hood added, "So the bunny stays in my basket during Drama? Or, if you want, I could magically transport him to your dorm room to nap. My basket can't handle anything much bigger than a bunny, but . . ."

"Maybe just keep him in the basket for now," Snowflake said quickly.

The two girls parted with Rapunzel at the grand staircase, then made a detour to get Snowflake's Handbook from her trunker.

"Okay, then. Let's go be theatrical!" Red Riding Hood said at last. With a dramatic flourish of her red cape, she led the way upstairs, her basket swinging gently from one arm.

Drama

As she and Red entered the auditorium, Snowflake fell silent, awestruck by its grimmazing architectural beauty. Its ceiling was painted with colorful scenes from various plays, and rows and rows of velvet chairs for the audience to sit in covered its carpeted floor. Box seats carved with cherubs and embellished with gold leaf jutted out along the walls, providing seating for any extra-special guests.

The stage itself was at the far end of the auditorium and had fancy blue velvet curtains edged with gold braid, fringe, and tassels. There were some desk chairs and random props scattered around on its wooden floor.

Red Riding Hood nudged Snowflake and nodded toward something that looked like a little doll riding atop a butterfly that was buzzing around the stage. "See, over there?" she said. "That's Mr. Thumb and his butterfly buddy, Schmetterling — that's the German word for butterfly. They were both actors and traveled all over Grimmlandia before coming to teach Drama here at the Academy. They're famous."

Mr. Thumb, who was no bigger than . . . well . . . a *thumb*, suddenly flew across the auditorium to hover in the air only a couple of feet from Snowflake's nose. He wore a hat made from an oak leaf and a thistledown jacket. Together, he and the iridescent orange-and-black monarch butterfly he rode made a striking sight.

After consulting the little vellum paper list he held in his small gloved hands, Mr. Thumb glanced up at Red and Snowflake. "Ah, Red Riding Hood! And who is this?"

"Snowflake," said Snowflake, introducing herself. "Both of us used to have Scrying fourth period. But since Ms. Wicked's gone, Ms. Jabberwocky reassigned us here."

"Good to have you! The more the merrier!" Mr. Thumb's voice was as tiny as he was, so he used a silver thimble as a bullhorn to make himself heard.

Red Riding Hood smiled. "Yeah, with more students, we can put on even bigger productions now."

Once everyone had gathered in the velvet seats closest to the stage, Mr. Thumb began class. "Welcome, students, new and old," he told them. "Today we will work on improvisation. That means acting without any preparation or planning. So I'll give you a setup, and you'll just jump right in, *improvising* a short scene."

Glancing at his list, he called, "Come onstage, Red Riding Hood, Wolfgang, and Snowflake. You'll go first."

Red Riding Hood left her basket in the care of a friend named Polly, but Snowflake took her Handbook along, just in case. Then Red, Wolfgang, and Snowflake climbed up onstage.

Mr. Thumb shouted, "Pretend you're in the Grimm History of Barbarians and Dastardlies class. Your teacher, Mr. Hump-Dumpty, announces a pop quiz. What do you do?"

"Cry?" Snowflake blurted out. The other students laughed and even Mr. Thumb smiled. Maybe taking part in this class wouldn't be so bad.

"Okay. Cue. Begin!" instructed the teacher.

Red Riding Hood and Wolfgang, who were both experienced actors, immediately launched into acting out a scene. And they made sure to include Snowflake. Right off, Wolfgang pretended to be Mr. Hump-Dumpty. So naturally, Red Riding Hood and Snowflake took on the role of students, which wasn't all that hard, since they actually were!

As others in the class looked on, Wolfgang picked up a yardstick lying among some other random props. Then, in imitation of Mr. Hump-Dumpty (who was basically an enormous egg with a face, arms, and legs), he leaned back, stuck out his stomach, and tucked in his chin to make himself look round.

Meanwhile, Red and Snowflake set two wooden chairs that were onstage side by side, and sat as if in a classroom. Wolfgang began to walk around, tapping the yardstick on the floor in the same way Mr. Hump-Dumpty often tapped his snazzy walking stick. Abruptly he stopped and pointed it at the two girls. "All right, class, today we're having a pop quiz! The purpose being to eggzamine eggsactly how much you know."

Many students out in the audience couldn't help laughing or applauding his imitation. It was spot-on!

Snowflake raised her hand. "I hate tests," she said, just being honest.

"Who doesn't?" said Red Riding Hood, nodding.

"Never fear," Wolfgang said in a teacher-y voice. "There's eggsellent information in your Handbooks that can help you get over your eggzam worries. Take a look."

"Really?" Snowflake did as he'd suggested. Holding her Handbook in the crook of one arm, she pushed the oval GA logo on the front of it with an index finger, saying, "Grimm Academy Handbook." You had to make clear what you wanted to read about before opening the Handbook, because it could change its text to reflect whatever class you were in.

Wolfgang and Red continued acting, but Snowflake forgot all about them as she flipped to the back of the book.

There, she found *test taking* in the index. When she pressed her finger on the words, a bubble rose to float in front of her. Words inside it read: *Test-Taking Tips to Relieve Anxiety.*

What do you know? Wolfgang hadn't just made up that stuff he'd said while pretending to be Mr. Hump-Dumpty!

"Last-minute cramming?" Wolfgang asked her, in his teacher voice.

Snowflake snapped to attention, only then remembering they were in the middle of doing a scene. "Oh, uh, no, sir. Just reading suggestions to relieve test-taking anxiety."

"Do give us some eggzamples," Wolfgang invited. "I'm sure other students will find such tips beneficial."

"Uh, okay." Snowflake decided to skip the most obvious test-taking tip: *Study.* "Here's a good one." She read it aloud: *"Don't panic if you don't know the answer to a question. If you blank on something, just move on to another part of the test."*

Following her lead, Red picked up an invisible test. She gazed at it, her eyes bugging out to demonstrate what *not* to do. Then she froze and looked around with a panicked expression that was so comical, even Snowflake laughed.

"Here's another tip," Snowflake went on. *"If you notice you are not thinking clearly, set the test aside and take a few slow deep breaths to help clear your mind and reduce your stress."* She proceeded to ball up a pretend test, toss it over one shoulder, and then draw a happy, relieved breath.

The audience laughed.

"I think you may have misinterpreted that tip," noted Wolfgang. "You still have to take the test."

"Yes, Mr. Hump-Dumpty," Red and Snowflake replied with comically woeful expressions.

"One last tip," said Snowflake. *"Pay attention to your test, not to what others are doing."*

Immediately, Red hopped up and went over to Wolfgang. "All finished, Mr. Hump-Dumpty! I think I aced it," she said, handing him her imaginary test.

Snowflake glanced up at Red and Wolfgang from her own pretend test and made an exaggerated "worried" face. Looking out at the audience, she wailed, "I'm doomed!" Then she practically fell out of her chair in a pretend faint. The class roared with laughter.

With a feeling of triumph, Snowflake straightened and shut her Handbook. *Snap!*

The audience clapped and cheered as the three actors bowed. Snowflake couldn't believe how much fun that scene had been. She'd heard that Red Riding Hood and Wolfgang had won the leads in the two most recent school plays and it was no wonder. They were good!

"Nicely done! I like how you included the Handbook, yardstick, and chairs as impromptu props," noted Mr. Thumb.

Snowflake was practically glowing as she, Red, and Wolfgang left the stage. Though they'd poked fun at those test-taking tips, she wondered if they could actually help her. Maybe she'd give them a shot for real sometime during an actual test.

They'd barely taken their seats together in the audience when a big bird whooshed from the hall into the auditorium. Several students pointed, squinting up at the creature. "How did that woodpecker get in here?" "I think it's a parrot." "No, look at that beak. It's a giant hummingbird!"

Their flying visitor swooped lower. "I'm a sprite, fools! Name's Jack Frost."

So this was the gold spinner! thought Snowflake. He had a beak, er, *nose* shaped like a carrot and wore a tasseled knit cap, sweater, and scarf. His breath came in frosty puffs when he spoke. Although he was considerably larger than Mr. Thumb, Jack Frost was still small. About the size of the bunny calmly sleeping in Red Riding Hood's basket.

"Well, Mr. Frost, we are conducting a class here!" Tom Thumb bullhorned at him. "Please go away."

"Excuuuse me!" the visitor huffed in a tone that indicated he wasn't at all sorry for interrupting. "Principal R said I can drop into classes to test students for talent in spinning straw into gold whenever I wish. In fact, I have a signed note from him to that effect!" Jack Frost whipped out a little rolled-up piece of paper and presented it to the teacher.

After studying it, Mr. Thumb sighed. "Class, it appears that Mr. Frost does indeed have permission to administer a test as he pleases."

Mr. Thumb reluctantly yielded the class, and the sprite took over. Flying back and forth above the edge of the stage, he gazed out at the students. "As you may have heard, I am looking for a very special trainee. Someone with the right talent to assist me in spinning the principal's magic straw into gold." He glanced over at the teacher. "To save time, I will test your entire class at once."

Mr. Thumb sighed. "Fine. Please be quick about it. I'll be backstage."

Snowflake slumped behind the student in front of her. *Tests, ugh.* The other students began grumbling, too.

"We've already tried spinning the straw and failed," someone protested.

"Yeah, why should we have to be tested again?" another called out.

"Because my test is new and better, and the results may be different," said Jack Frost.

It turned out to be an odd test. First, he instructed them to hold out a hand, palm up. Next, a container of water was passed around, and they each had to pour about a spoonful of it into their upturned palm, then wait to learn the next step.

"Huh? How is this going to help him find someone who can spin straw into gold?" Red Riding Hood wondered aloud as she poured water into her hand.

"No clue," said Snowflake. After doing the same and passing the pitcher on, she peered at the water in her palm. It had particles of something in it. Dust?

"Everyone ready?" When all the students nodded, Jack Frost went on. "Now close your hand into a fist. After I count to five, you can open it." Everyone did as instructed.

"Okay, one, two, three, four, five . . . open sesame!" shouted Jack Frost.

All around Snowflake, she heard disappointed or annoyed murmurs as students checked their palms. "Yeah, just like I thought — nothing happened." "Except the water in my hand leaked out onto my lap!" "This test is so lame." "Whatever!"

Slowly, Snowflake opened her hand, palm up. There was no gold in her palm, but . . . there was something else. Something weird.

"Yep, still water," she heard Red say from beside her. Rubbing her hands together briskly to dry them off, Red leaned over to Wolfgang.

"Same," he said, playfully flicking the water in his palm toward her.

Laughing, Red leaned Snowflake's way to duck the spray of water. "Hey! What's that?" she shouted, drawing everyone's attention as she stared into Snowflake's open palm.

In a nanosecond, Jack Frost shot across the auditorium to hover in front of Snowflake. "Puffin' permafrost!" he exclaimed when he saw what her palm held. Everywhere, students were standing and craning their necks to see.

Snowflake wasn't sure why everyone was getting so excited. She'd failed the test same as everyone else. She hadn't made gold. Instead, she held . . . a perfect blue-white snowflake as big as her entire hand.

"Look, it's cold!" someone shouted, pointing out the frosty air around it.

"But it isn't melting," noted another student.

"Cool!" pronounced Red.

Snowflake tried to shake off the snowflake. It came off all right, but it didn't fall to the floor. Instead, it began whirling and twirling in the air around her like some kind of crazy, six-sided pancake, leaving a trail of magic sparkles in its wake.

"What's your name?" Jack Frost demanded eagerly.

"Snowflake."

"I know it's a snowflake, but what's your name?"

"That *is* my name," she told him.

Her mind had begun to race with wild, worried thoughts. Was making a snowflake a "horrid" thing to do? Had her bangs been curly when she was a baby? Was she about to find out she really was the Little Girl Who Had a Little Curl? *Stop it!* she silently hissed at herself. Making a snowflake was hardly proof that that particular nursery rhyme was hers. If anything, it might show the opposite since the rhyme didn't mention snowflakes at all. But then who was she?

Itching to get away from all the attention — as well as the snowflake — she stood. The flake still dipped and soared around her doing sparkly acrobatics. It just wouldn't leave her alone! And to complicate matters, her bunny — no, he was *not* hers, she reminded herself — started banging around inside Red Riding Hood's basket.

Suddenly, the bunny-powered basket hopped out into the main aisle and bounded away with the bunny inside. *Boing! Boing!*

Too stunned to act, all the other students looked on as Red and Snowflake took off after the bouncing basket.

"Hey, wait!" shouted Jack Frost. He zipped through the air after the girls.

Outside the auditorium, the bunny boinged out of the basket and hopped away. As Red Riding Hood stopped to scoop up her basket, Snowflake continued after the bunny. Despite the trouble he caused, the cute critter was growing on her. She needed to make sure he would be okay.

She was so focused on trying to recapture him that she didn't notice she'd failed to rid herself of the pesky six-sided snowflake she'd made. It was still following her!

10

Winter Wonderland

Snowflake finally caught up to the bunny outside the library, which had relocated itself to the first floor of Pink Castle today. When she set her Handbook on the floor and picked up the little guy, his heart was thumping wildly.

"Why'd you hop off like that, silly?" she asked. She cuddled him to her chest, stroking his soft fur. "I guess that's just what rabbits do, huh?"

He nuzzled her hand in reply, snuggling closer. Since the period hadn't actually let out yet, the halls around her were empty and quiet. Then a voice piped up.

"Honk!" It was the library's goose-head knob. "You again!" it exclaimed. "You owe me, remember? You'll have to answer two riddles to get in this time!"

Snowflake pursed her lips in annoyance. "Sorry, but I'm kind of in a hurry again. The Hickory Dickory Dock clock's going to bong in about fifteen minutes, and I have stuff I need to get done in there before my next class."

The gooseknob glared at her. If it had had an actual goose body, she felt sure it would've crossed its wings and tapped a foot impatiently.

She sighed. "All right, but make the riddles easy. Please? Like I said, I'm in a hurry."

"Honk! Seems to me you're always in a hurry," observed the knob. It eyed the bunny, and then posed this question: "How do you make a hop optimistic?"

"Um . . . change it to hoptimistic?" she replied quickly.

"Ha-ha-ha!" the knob honk-laughed. "I never thought of that! I was actually going for 'Add an e on the end of *hop* to make the word *hope*.' But I like your answer, so I'll accept it."

"Really? Thanks." Snowflake felt optimistically hopeful that the gooseknob would appreciate her creativity so much it would let her skip answering a second riddle. But no such luck.

"And now for my next question," announced the knob. "The opposite of a sad bunny is what kind of bunny?"

"A hopposite one?" she said, adopting the same strategy she'd used to come up with her first answer.

Only this time the knob didn't laugh. "That doesn't even make sense," it scolded her. "You're just being a lazy thinker now. Try again."

She let out a little huff, but then tried to puzzle things out. "Well, the opposite of sad is glad, or cheerful, or happy," she mused aloud. "*Hmm.* Happy. Is the opposite of a sad bunny a *hoppy* one?"

Snick! Without another word, the gooseknob turned back into a plain round knob. Right away, a rectangle that was several feet taller than Snowflake and about four feet wide magically drew itself on the wall around the knob. That became the library door, decorated with low-relief carvings of nursery-rhyme characters like Little Bo Peep and her sheep.

With book and bunny now cradled in her arms, Snowflake turned the knob and dashed for her makeshift room in Section *F.* Luckily, Ms. Goose was nowhere in sight. And there were only a few students around as she made a couple of stops along the way. In the *B* section, she picked up a box full of shredded paper for a bunny bathroom. And in the *D* section, she snagged a dish of drinking water for the critter.

Darting into her room at last, she laid out everything she thought the bunny would need and got it settled. Then she sat on her high feather bed, pondering Jack Frost's "test."

Suddenly she heard a noise outside her room. *Swish! Swish!*

What in Grimmlandia was that? She climbed down from the top mattress and went to open the door a crack, barely wide enough to peek out. *Huh?* There, levitating in midair outside her door, was . . . the snowflake from Drama! She thought she'd escaped it, yet here it was, back again. Had another student entered the library and let it in without noticing?

"Go away," she whispered to it. "I don't need you drawing attention to me and my secret room, thank you very much."

Instead of obeying, the hand-size snowflake began to whirl around in excited little circles and bump against the door, as if overjoyed to see her again. Snowflake quickly stepped out of her room, closing it behind her.

She flicked both hands at the flake. "Shoo! Go find some snowflake friends and make a snowball or something!"

Just then, Rapunzel and Cinda walked by, carrying papers and pens. Cinda's roommate, a shapeshifting mermaid named Mermily, was with them.

"Hi," Cinda said to Snowflake.

"Hi. You guys here to do homework or something?" she asked, trying to sound casual. It wasn't easy to do. From the corner of her eye, she could see the snowflake on an empty shelf behind the girls, rolling around on its edges like a six-sided wheel. Then it started doing flips and hops, obviously trying to get her attention.

"Our whole Grimm History class is in the library," Cinda told her. "Mr. Hump-Dumpty is bringing everyone here to research Dastardlies today."

"Guess I'm right where I need to be, then," said Snowflake. "I've got History next period."

Before she could say anything more, the snowflake zoomed over, whooshing around the girls and sending sparkles into the air.

Snowflake frowned, but the other girls giggled in delight.

Thump! Thump!

Oh, fuzzbobbers. Now she could hear that bunny hopping around inside her room. Her companions looked at her door.

"What was that?" asked Rapunzel.

"I didn't hear anything," Snowflake fibbed. If the girls pushed that door open and discovered she was staying here, she'd probably get in big trouble.

"So . . . Dastardlies, huh? Can I start researching with you?" she asked, ushering everyone toward the next aisle and away from her secret room. "Since I'm already here, I might as well get going on the assignment early. We should probably head for Section *D*." She hurried in that direction, hoping the bunny didn't make too much mischief while she was gone.

As the four girls headed for *D*, the annoying snowflake caught up to them again. Mermily pointed it out. "Is that your magical charm?" she asked Snowflake as the flake gracefully swooped around them.

"What? No! It just keeps hanging around me." Snowflake didn't tell them she'd accidentally *made* the flake in Drama class. Instead, she shot off toward the library exit, planning to shoo it out into the hall. Curious, Cinda, Rapunzel, and Mermily followed.

Cinda flipped her blond hair over one shoulder as she caught up to Snowflake. "Are you sure it isn't your charm?" she asked. "I didn't think my glass slippers were my charm at first, either. I wasn't convinced till they started dancing me around at Prince Awesome's ball and helped me find a hidden map."

"Took me a while to figure out about my charm, too," said Rapunzel as they all paused just inside the library door. "Not until my comb started resizing itself and changing shape at my command did I know for sure it was mine."

"I haven't gotten a charm yet," Mermily said, sounding a little sad. "Most kids wait *years* before they get one, though. And magical charms only come to those who are good of heart."

Cinda gave her a quick hug. "Which means you'll get yours any day now." Mermily started to smile at her, but then a look of surprise filled her face as the sparkly flake swooped past her nose.

It zoomed twice around their group before landing lightly upon Snowflake's head like a flat hat. "Hey! Stop that!" she yelled. She ducked from under it, then stuck out her hand and batted it away.

Snap! When her hand made contact, the snowflake grew a stem! The stem slipped itself into her palm, and her fingers automatically wrapped around it. A startled hush fell over the four girls as they stared at the snowflake-on-a-stick she now clasped.

Cinda clapped gleefully, bouncing on her toes. "See? It must be your charm."

"A white six-sided pancake flake on a lollipop stick?" Snowflake said doubtfully.

The other girls laughed. "Not a lollipop," Rapunzel said, squinting at it critically. "It's more like a . . . a wand."

Mermily's eyes lit up. "That's it! It's a *magic wand*!"

Snowflake gazed at the snowflake-topped stick in wonder. Her fingers folded more firmly around the wand — if that's what it really was. It fit her hand perfectly. She remembered Ms. Goose's remark about how one day she would find something in the library that *fit*. Snowflake had thought she meant a tale, not a *thing*. *Then you'll be filled with recognition. You'll just know.*

She shook her head. "Like Mermily said, most charms take a long time to come to students, and I've only been here a week. I'm not so sure about the *good of heart* part, either."

"Don't be silly," said Cinda. "Of course you're good of heart."

Snowflake shrugged. Cinda didn't know about the trouble Snowflake had caused at her old school.

"There's one way to find out if it's your charm. Try to make it do something magical," suggested Rapunzel.

"Here? In the library?" asked Snowflake. The others all nodded.

"Um, okay." Standing back from them, she waved the wand in the air in a figure-eight shape. Nothing happened.

"Try giving it instructions. In rhyme," Cinda prompted.

Snowflake thought for a minute.

"Bestow snow," she commanded. She waved it again. It began to snow *in the library*! But only on her, Cinda, Rapunzel, and Mermily.

"It's like standing in the shower, only with snow instead of water coming down," said Mermily. She stepped out of the snow shower for a moment, and then back inside again.

Cinda and Rapunzel began scooping up the big fat flakes of snow at their feet to make snowballs. Falling snow always seems to make people happy, thought Snowflake. It had perked up her spirits, too!

Tap. Tap. Tap. Mr. Hump-Dumpty, the egg-shaped History teacher walked up to them. He wore an orange tunic and tapped his snazzy walking stick on the library floor with every other step, just as Wolfgang had done during Drama when he'd imitated him. The egg-teacher's shell was cracked in a few places, including across his forehead. Now it cracked a little more as he knit his brow in concern.

"Snow is not allowed in the library, girls! Wet floors are eggstra slippery and can be eggstremely, eggcessively dangerous. So please take your snow with you out the nearest eggxit!" He pointed the end of his walking stick toward the library door.

"Sorry, sir," said Snowflake. She thought it was a little strange when he didn't appear surprised that it was snowing indoors. But magic was pretty much an everyday occurrence at the Academy. He'd probably seen plenty of things just as unusual!

Nice Ice

The snow shower followed the girls out into the hall. Rapunzel smiled. "Can you make it stop?" she asked Snowflake. "My hair's getting a little damp."

"I'll try." Snow waved the wand again, but the snow didn't stop.

"Maybe say more magic words?" suggested Mermily.

"And make them a rhyming command again," added Cinda.

Snowflake pointed the wand toward an open window along the hall. "Go, snow!"

The small snow shower immediately whooshed out the window. The girls hurried over and gazed outside, watching it blow across the lawn.

"Think it'll just keep going forever?" Rapunzel asked.

"Who knows?" Snowflake replied.

Soon the snow was over the Once Upon River, halfway between Heart Island and Maze Island. That gave Snowflake an idea. She poked her flakey wand out the window and waved it, saying:

"Snow, turn to ice, quick as a wink
And make us a perfect skating rink!"

The snow halted and dropped into the river. A small patch of ice formed where it fell and proceeded to spread outward.

"Uh-oh, what if it turns the whole river to ice?" fretted Mermily. "I like swimming out there."

Luckily, the ice patch stopped growing once it had become a small island.

"A skating rink!" squealed Cinda.

"I've never tried skating," said Rapunzel.

"Me either, but there's a first time for everything," said Snowflake.

Mermily grinned. "So what are we waiting for? Mr. Hump-Dumpty gave us permission to eggxit, right? Let's go!"

Snowflake followed her friends — no, *acquaintances* — as they stashed their stuff in their trunkers and dashed outside. By then, other students had noticed the ice patch in the river and were leaning out classroom windows to get a better view.

"What is it?" Snow White called down to the girls.

"Looks like an island of ice!" Dragonbreath yelled from one window over.

"Yeah! Snowflake made it with her magical charm!" Rapunzel called up to them.

"Grimmtabulous!" Rose shouted from a window on the second floor. Beyond her, they could hear the teacher, Ms. Queenharts, shouting about how shouting was unmannerly.

A new, low sound reached their ears. It was the Hickory Dickory Dock clock bonging that it was time for fifth-period classes to begin. The girls' shoulders slumped, and they started to return indoors.

But then, Prince Awesome bounded out of Pink Castle and called, "Principal R heard about the ice patch and canceled fifth and sixth periods so we can explore it!"

Whoops went up from students all over the Academy. Everyone disappeared from the windows and flooded outside. Snowflake, Rapunzel, Cinda, and Mermily scurried to the riverbank and hopped into a swan boat. Red Riding Hood, Rose, Goldilocks, and Mary Mary caught up and took a boat right next to them.

"When we get to the island, I'll transport skates for everyone with my basket," Red Riding Hood called. Her basket was safely looped over her arm again.

"Good thing — we'll need them!" Cinda told Red as they pushed away from shore.

Red Riding Hood laughed. As her group got ready to shove off, she called across to Snowflake, "Hey, where's your bunny?"

"In my room," Snowflake replied without thinking. Then she sent Mary Mary a guilty glance. Why she should feel guilty, she wasn't sure. Because it was Mary Mary's grumpiness that had pushed her out of sharing that girl's dorm room in Emerald Tower in the first place. Snowflake was not going to stay where she wasn't wanted!

Mary Mary scowled as her boat kept pace with Snowflake's. Her eyes still had that strange glazed look from earlier as she glared at Snowflake's wand. "So that's your charm?" she snapped. "Humpf! I thought those only came to students who were good of heart."

Snowflake drew in a sharp breath, feeling like she'd been stung by some of those albino bees she'd stirred up back at her village.

Rapunzel sent Mary Mary a disapproving look. "Well, that was kind of snippy, even for *you*."

"I don't know what you're talking about," the contrary girl sniffed.

Oddly enough, Snowflake had a feeling Mary Mary really didn't know she'd been acting extra rude lately. Did it have something to do with that new glaze in her gaze? Or was it possible that her contrariness was simply a defense mechanism so she wouldn't feel hurt if no one wanted to be her friend? That was something Snowflake could understand. She pushed people away on purpose, too. *Sigh.* At some point, they were going to have to talk this out. Even though she'd really rather avoid friendship drama. Especially when she had her own stuff to deal with!

"I'm sure Mary Mary didn't mean to be mean," Cinda said as the girls paddled farther out into the river, pulling ahead of the other boats. Mermily nodded, sending Snowflake a concerned look.

"Forget her. Let's go have some fun!" With enthusiasm, Rapunzel dug her paddle deep in the water, and their boat shot forward.

They rowed out to the middle of the Once Upon River and were the first of all the boats to reach the icy shore of the new island Snowflake had made. Quickly, they disembarked.

The minute Snowflake stepped onto the ice, she began to slip and slide. "Whoa!" she said as she nearly fell. Her companions were grabbing onto one another, trying to keep from falling, too. While the girls slipped and slid on the ice, more boats landed and students got out.

Snowflake had been gazing down at her feet as they began to slide out from under her yet again when a strong hand took hold of her arm. She looked up into a pair of sparkly green eyes. Prince Dragonbreath's eyes.

"Thanks for the save," she said after he steadied her.

"You're welcome." He smiled at her, then let go of her arm.

Immediately, she started to slip again. "Whoa!" Reaching out, she grabbed both of his hands while still managing to hold on to her wand. Suddenly, she felt an odd added weight beneath her feet. She glanced down. "Hey!" she exclaimed, "Something's happening to my slippers! They're turning into . . ."

"Ice skates! My boots are, too!" said Dragonbreath, looking down. Delighted giggles and exclamations sounded all around them as everyone else's footwear was magically transformed into skates, too.

"How is this happening?" wondered Snowflake. She relaxed her grip on his hands a bit, but still didn't let go.

"I think it's this ice you made," Dragonbreath told her. "It must be magic. The minute you step on it, your boots, slippers, or whatever transform into skates!"

A thrill shot through Snowflake. *Her* magic had done this? The two of them watched as students bladed away on their newly-made skates. When Red zoomed past, her bright crimson cape billowed out behind her. Rapunzel soon caught up to her and glided expertly around the rink, her dark hair whipping in the breeze. But she had said she'd never skated before!

Pleased murmurs of "I didn't know if I could do this, but it's easy!" reached Snowflake's ears as more and more students took to the ice wearing magic skates.

As Cinda, Snow White, and Mermily skated by arm in arm, they called to her. "Grab on!"

Snowflake finally let go of Dragonbreath's hands. To her surprise, she skated smoothly out onto the ice on her own. It really *was* easy. Were the skates magical, too?

She caught Cinda's hand and soon picked up speed, zooming around the rink with her and the others. The skates did have magic in them, she decided. She'd never skated before, and she couldn't have learned *this* fast. In no time at all, she was performing twirls and figure eights, even jumps!

Before long, Mr. Hump-Dumpty joined the students on the island. Not to skate, though. It seemed he was concerned for their safety and had appointed himself security eggspert. He stood on the outskirts of the ice and pointed his snazzy walking stick at students every so often. "Slow down! Not so close to the edge, boys! No triple jumps, girls! Everyone skate counterclockwise. No eggceptions!"

Snowflake paused in the middle of the rink after a while to catch her breath and watch the other skaters circling her. Wouldn't it be fun to add more icy features to this island? she thought. Her mind began to form pictures of a castle that could stand at the rink's center, while students skated around and around it. She knew exactly how it should look.

Could the wand execute her idea for her? There was only one way to find out. She pointed her wand toward the spot where she wanted her castle to stand, then chanted:

"Wand, please use your magic powers
To build a castle with four towers!"

A loud cracking, crunching sound came from the very spot where she'd been pointing her snowflake wand. Then, *whoosh!* An ice castle shot up through the island's center to stand several stories tall.

"Nice," Snowflake murmured to herself, smiling. Built exactly as she'd imagined it, it was square at the base, three stories high, and had one turreted tower at each of its four corners. And all was made of white ice that glistened in the sunlight.

"Careful! Watch out, everyone!" Mr. Hump-Dumpty yelled when he first saw the castle shoot up. But after a moment he proclaimed it, "An eggsellent addition to the island!"

Students began skating around the castle, oohing and aahing. As pleased as Snowflake was with her creation, ideas for small changes and improvements were already forming in her head. She waved her wand again causing a fifth central tower and crenellated battlements to form. After brief consideration, she sloped the roof more, giving it a cute upward curl all along its bottom edge. Lastly, she added heart-shaped windows in each tower.

"Nice work!" called Dragonbreath, skating over.

"It's gorgeous!" enthused Cinda as she and Snow White slid up on Snowflake's other side. More students exclaimed over her castle and shouted out compliments, too.

"I couldn't have done it without this magic wand," Snowflake disclaimed.

"But it was your idea," Cinda insisted. "You *designed* it."

"Yeah, you and your wand worked as a team!" Snow White declared.

Snowflake smiled as happiness filled her. She and her wand did make a pretty good team. She had always loved designing buildings in her mind or on paper, but she'd never been able to actually build them until her magical charm came along. It was like a grimmazing tool, moving ice blocks into position that normally would be too heavy or unwieldy for her to even budge. She was still the one who decided how to put those blocks together to make things, though. The ideas were truly hers.

"Three cheers for Snowflake and her Ice Island!" shouted Dragonbreath, punching a fist in the air. In response, students whooped and clapped enthusiastically.

Snowflake sent him a smile. "Ice Island. I like the sound of that."

"Ice melts eventually," she heard Mary Mary mutter somewhere behind her.

True, thought Snowflake. But they could all enjoy the island for as long as it lasted, right? Already, ideas for designing the *inside* of the castle had begun to dance in her mind. She could hardly wait to try them out!

12

Jack Frost

Unnoticed by the students whizzing around on the island rink, Jack Frost sat atop the ice castle roof, thinking hard. He'd lost track of this Snowflake girl after the incident in her Drama class. Naturally, he'd wasted no time in flitting over to the island when he'd seen her and these other students boating out here.

So, she'd created all this, hmm? Who was she? And where did she get such powers?

He lay on his back, crossed one pointy boot over his opposite knee, and slid down the castle's sloped roof. It curved upward along its bottom edge, causing him to go swooping up into the air when he reached the end. *Whee!* He flew back up to the roof's peak and slid down again, his mind working all the while on the question of which character in literature this girl might actually be. Something she didn't even seem to know herself.

Snowflake. Snow. Flakes. Ice. Castle. Ice castle. Snow . . .

Suddenly, it came to him. *Frosty icicle bicycles!* He'd guessed who she was!

Jack Frost dug his boot heels into the ice roof and skidded to a stop. Then he shot up in the air and did head-over-heel flips around the central ice tower till he was dizzy with joy. Because Snowflake, as she called herself, was going be his ticket to evil stardom!

From high above the skating rink below, he watched her help Prince Foulsmell stand after he'd fallen on the ice. *Hmm,* that wasn't something the most evil person left in Grimmlandia should be doing. If she was as clueless about her destiny as she seemed to be, she had to be told before she went too far over to the good side.

And he was just the one to break the good, er, *evil* news to her!

13

Ice Castle

Snowflake gazed up at her ice castle's five pointed towers. The exterior was done for now, but excitement flurried inside her as she continued contemplating how she might design the *inside* of the castle. First, however, she needed a way in. She lifted her wand. Using its magic, she traced an outline of a shapely arched door in the center of the castle's front wall. But try as she might to pry it open, the door stayed firmly shut.

Just then, Prince Dragonbreath whizzed by. He and some other boys had begun to play ice hockey with a puck and sticks that one of them had brought over from the Academy. *Whack!* He passed the puck off to another player.

Noticing her struggle, he called to her. "Need some help?" He skated backward until he was in front of the castle. "Stand aside," he warned her as he came even with the outlined door. She glided out of the way right in the nick of time.

Zzzt! He let out a stream of fiery dragon breath. The fire traced the outline she'd drawn exactly. Cutting all the way through the thick ice, it zipped up one side, across the top, and down the other in mere seconds.

Taken by surprise, Snowflake gasped and cringed from the fire in fear. Luckily, Dragonbreath didn't notice. Already he'd turned his attention back to the hockey puck, which had sailed his way once more. He gave it a good whack and then headed off to continue the game just as a door-size chunk of ice fell outward from the castle like a drawbridge. *Ka-chunk!*

Alone, Snowflake stepped inside her castle for the very first time. Her skates instantly transformed back into slippers. There was to be no skating indoors apparently. Mr. Hump-Dumpty would approve of this precaution, she thought with a smile.

She could see her breath in here. It was chilly, but for some reason, the cold air felt comfy and cozy to her. A good "fit," as Ms. Goose might say.

The inside of the castle was just one big hollow space right now. But she had grand plans for what she could do with it. Namely, add balconies, chandeliers, knight statues, and circular staircases, all carved from ice!

Ka-chunk! Ka-chunk! With a wave of her wand, she caused blocks of ice to magically form, reshape, and move wherever she wanted them to go. She created stairs, passageways, and many rooms, all dusted with bright, beautiful sparkles. Taking a break, she gazed around. A thrill swept through her. With the help of her wand, she'd done this. And it was beautiful!

She climbed up the grand staircase she'd made to the central tower and stood at its heart-shaped window to gaze out over the ice. Though it was late afternoon, the sun still shone brightly. Her island looked like a brilliant white winter wonderland!

Things were looking up for her. Maybe she had finally found the building material she'd needed all along to real-ize her dreams of becoming a real architect, she thought happily. And that material, of course, was *ice*.

"Too bad this will all melt away soon," she said to her snowflake wand. Her voice echoed through the ice cavern.

"Who said it has to?" said a small voice.

Snowflake looked at her wand in surprise. Could it talk? But then the sprite Jack Frost appeared, hovering in the air outside her castle window. It was *his* voice she'd heard.

She stepped back. "Ice melts — that's all there is to it," she replied.

"Not necessarily. Not if you stay on this island and use your powers to stop it from happening, Your Snowiness! I mean, Your Queenliness!" To her astonishment, he touched down on the windowsill and bowed low to her.

Snowflake sent him a quizzical look. What in Grimmlandia was he talking about? "I'm not a queen. I'm just a girl."

"Wrong! I know what I'm talking about. My test found you," Jack Frost said confidently.

"But even if you're right about me being a queen — and I really do think you're mistaken — I can't spin straw into gold. I already tried."

"Bah! That stuff about finding someone to help me create gold was only a cunning trick of mine," said Jack Frost. "Your principal could turn that straw to gold on his own, the fool. He just doesn't know how to use his own power, which between you and me is fueled by, guess what? His anger! *Ha-ha-ha!*"

He spun around in the air until he became a giddy blur, then righted himself and got serious. "As for your gift, it's obviously snow and ice. And mine's frost. Working together, we could be invincible! We'll turn Grimmlandia — and maybe even the Nothingterror and other realms yet to be discovered — into wintery lands that we'll rule!" In his excitement, he did a loop-the-loop spin in midair, leaving behind a corkscrew trail of glittery frost.

Growing anxious, Snowflake rolled her wand between her fingers. "Wait. I don't get it. Your test . . ."

"Haven't you guessed who you are?" he went on before she could finish. "Here's a hint. You're a fairy-tale character, an evil one." He paused dramatically, then blurted, "The Snow Queen!"

Snowflake gasped and stumbled back a step. "The *evil* Snow Queen?" She'd heard the Snow Queen's tale long ago in school, but had never actually read it herself. She'd sort of forgotten about it. Her heart hammered in her chest. Could it be true? "No! That can't have anything to do with me. I'm a nursery-rhyme character," she protested, shaking her head. "Maybe not a good one, but nothing as villainous as the Snow Queen, I'm sure."

"Read my lips," said Jack Frost. Speaking slowly and loudly, he said, "You. Are. The. Snow. Queen." He did a little happy dance on the newel post at the top of the stairs she'd created, then slid down the stair banister and back up it again. *Whee!*

In her eagerness to convince him (and maybe herself, too) that he was wrong, Snowflake stretched the truth a bit. "I know for a fact that I'm the horrid girl in the Henry Wadsworth Longfellow rhyme. You know how it goes? 'There was a little girl / Who had a little curl / Right in the middle of her forehead / And when she was good / She was very, very good / But when she was bad — she was horrid.' That's me!"

Jack Frost stood firmly on the banister and folded his arms. "Nope. Just look around you. Your icy powers prove I'm right. There's no mention of ice or snow in that nursery rhyme. Besides, I make it my business to know about all evil characters. You're the Snow Queen from the Hans Christian Andersen tale."

She cocked her head. "It's not a Grimm fairy tale?"

"Humpf! And you can be glad of that. I'm no fan of those talentless Grimm brothers. They didn't include me in their tales, and they locked me in a snow globe!" Jack flitted closer until he was directly in front of her nose. "So what do you say, Queenie? Shall we work together so I can . . . um, I mean *you* can rule as you're intended to? C'mon. Turn to the evil side — it's so much more fun than being good."

She didn't want what this sprite was saying to be true! "No! No! No!" As she spoke, she accidently waved her wand in emphasis.

Screech! Crunch! Chunks of ice began moving here and there to create new features inside the castle. These weren't cute features, either, but strange and creepy ones. Were they born of her unsettled feelings? Or from her true nature? She shuddered as stalactites with monstrous faces formed on the ceiling and icy cobwebs wove themselves in high corners. She could feel her emotions slipping and sliding out of control. With his terrible news, Jack Frost had completely erased her pleasure in what had been, up to now, a perfect afternoon.

Just then, Dragonbreath called to her from outside. "Hey, Snowflake! Want me to add some more windows?"

Snowflake took great gulps of breath, trying to calm down as she went to the window again. There, she leaned out to see Dragonbreath on the ice below. "No, that's okay. Maybe later," she called back.

"Steer clear of him," Jack Frost advised from somewhere behind her. "Dragon fire is dangerous. Remember how he melted that door in seconds flat?"

"But that was only to help me," she protested, turning to look at the sprite as he floated above the banister.

"Still, if dragon fire can do that to your castle, imagine what it could do to you and your icy powers. Not to mention to me!" said Jack Frost, fanning the flames of fire fear in her mind.

This sprite was kind of right. Dragonbreath was all about fire, and she was all about ice. Talk about opposites! They weren't good for each other at all. They shouldn't be friends.

Dragonbreath had helped her today, but if he ever wanted to, he could melt whatever she built with a single puff of fiery breath. Which made him especially dangerous to an architect whose material was *ice*. No wonder she had always feared fire!

As she fretted, Jack Frost drifted happily around the inside of the castle. "This place will be the perfect lair for us to operate from," he said, returning to her after a couple of minutes.

"Lair? I don't need a lair because . . . because I'm not a villain!" She thrust out her arm, showing him her wand. "I — I have a magical charm, and they only come to those who're good of heart!" Still, deep inside, she feared Jack Frost was right. Because the tale of the Snow Queen . . . well . . . much as she hated to admit it, it *fit*.

"Haven't you ever heard of an *evil* charm?" he asked. "Like Ms. Wicked's crystal ball or her mirror, for instance?"

Was he right? She supposed it was proof of her true nature that she'd accidentally transformed her beautiful castle into something awful — an evil lair!

Totally freaking out now, Snowflake threw her snowflake wand at him. "Take it! If it's evil, I don't want any part of it. You can have the wand and go be evil on your own!" With those parting words, she ran down the ice stairs and out of the castle. Her slippers turned into skates again, and she zoomed off past all the laughing, playing students.

Anger and self-pity rose in her as she sped toward the swan boats. Why did this have to happen when things had been going so well the past couple of days? She'd been wrong to forget her number one rule and start getting to know and like some of these students. Those budding friendships would soon wither and die when everyone found out who she *really* was.

Her cheeks were flushed, and her heart was galloping away. "Calm down, calm down," she murmured to herself. Nothing good ever came from letting her emotions spiral out of control. She sensed that if she couldn't get a handle on them, something ghastly was going to happen.

Mermily came skating toward her. "Where are you going to in such a hurry?" she asked with a smile.

Obviously, that girl had no idea who she was talking to. Before Snowflake could warn her to get out of her way, it suddenly began to sleet. Everyone gazed up at the sky. The freezing rain was only falling over the island, she realized. She had a bad feeling about this. A bad feeling that whatever this meant, it was her fault!

"We've got to get out of here!" she told Mermily. Cupping her hands around her mouth, Snowflake yelled to the other students. "Get off the island. It's not safe!"

Mr. Hump-Dumpty's big eyes went wide. She felt bad for worrying him. But it worked like a charm.

"Scramble, everyone! Off the island!" the egg teacher boomed, waving his arms wildly. "Everyone eggxit to the boats. Eggscape while you can! Danger! Danger!"

Snowflake and Mermily rushed for the icy shore along with everyone else. Meanwhile, the freezing rain fell faster and faster. Cries of "Ow! Ow!" sounded as the sleet struck the skaters.

Snowflake started to help those around her into the swan-shaped boats. The moment they stepped off the island, the skates on their feet turned back into their original footwear. She guided Cinda into a boat, but was startled when the girl jerked and cried out, putting a hand to her cheek.

Prince Awesome rushed over to Cinda, asking, "What's wrong?"

"I — I don't know. It felt like something stung me," she told him. "It was just the sleet, I guess."

Snowflake stared at Cinda in concern . . . and watched the girl's blue eyes glaze over. Just like Mary Mary's had back in the garden. What did it mean?

"Want me to take you up to the office of the Doctor, the Nurse, and the Lady with the Alligator Purse when we get back to GA?" Awesome offered kindly.

In spite of how upset she was, Snowflake let out a nervous giggle. Because the Lady with the Alligator Purse was a funny name for a member of the Academy medical staff.

"What are you laughing at?" Cinda demanded, glaring at her. "You think my injury is funny?"

"Huh? No!" said Snowflake.

"No one would think that," Rapunzel tried to tell Cinda.

"Are you okay?" her roommate, Mermily, asked. She tried to give Cinda a hug, but Cinda pushed her away.

"Oh, just leave me alone, all of you!" complained the glass-slippered girl. "And by the way, I don't like the nickname Cinda. It's Cinderella from now on!"

With that, she jumped out of the boat and dashed off, leaving them all bewildered. After settling herself in a swan boat only big enough for one passenger, she rowed for the Academy on her own.

Prince Awesome rubbed the back of his neck, looking worried. "She's not usually like that," he commented to Foulsmell as the two boys climbed into the boat Cinda had abandoned and pushed off into the river.

Exactly, thought Snowflake, though she still didn't know what to make of the change that had come over Cinda. And Mary Mary before her!

She hopped into a boat with Rapunzel, Red Riding Hood, and Mermily. The minute they shoved off, the sleet stopped. Along with at least a dozen other student-filled swan boats, they rowed across the river toward the opposite bank where Grimm Academy stood. As they paddled, the girls in Snowflake's boat discussed Cinda's weird behavior.

Was it *my* fault? Because I laughed? Snowflake silently worried. Or maybe that had nothing to do with it. What if being an evil character meant you rubbed everyone the wrong way, no matter what you said or did? She didn't want to be the Snow Queen. Once again, she wondered how these girls — and everyone else at GA — would react when they found out her fairy-tale identity.

After they landed on the shore near Pink Castle, she watched Awesome catch up to Cinda, er, Cinderella. The two of them headed for the school drawbridge.

"Maybe *he* can talk to her and figure things out," said Rapunzel, nodding toward the pair.

"Yeah, maybe they had a fight or something earlier and she was already on edge and waiting to snap," Red Riding Hood suggested as they climbed out of their boat.

Snowflake didn't think that was it, however. After all, Cinderella now had the same glazed look in her eyes as Mary Mary. And as everyone filed back into the Academy, she heard some other students arguing or acting oddly and noticed that their eyes had become glazed, too. Had they been struck by those icy shards, like Cinda? And was it possible that Mary Mary had somehow been struck by a shard that day in the garden? Could Snowflake's icy evil Snow Queen powers really be causing this change in behavior?

Although she had come to really like her fellow students, she vowed to steer clear of them all in the future. For their sakes as much as hers. She wouldn't go to the Great Hall with everyone tonight to eat dinner. She would just hang out in her library hideaway and hope that would stop her from stirring up trouble — however unintentionally — from now on.

Speaking of the library, she wondered what that bunny had gotten up to while she was away. Had he been doing okay all day in her room? Or had he destroyed the place with his teeth and claws?

After hurrying into the school, she found the library again in two shakes of a bunny's tail, still on the first floor. Someone had left the door ajar, and she reached for the plain brass knob, eager to give it a twist and check on things. The knob morphed before she could sneak inside.

"Not so fast," snipped the goose-head knob. "It's riddle time. You're my best customer lately. What gives? Why are you spending so much time in the library?"

"Is that the riddle?"

"No."

"Well, please get on with it," she replied. "I've got stuff to do in the library. *Private* stuff."

The knob huffed and muttered something that sounded like, "Nobody ever tells me anything." Then it said more loudly, "Okay, here goes:

"Within my two walls are adventures galore.
Your two hands can unlock my door.
What am I?"

Two walls? What had only two walls? Snowflake wondered to herself. Searching for ideas, she looked around the hall. *Aha!* She snapped her fingers. "I know. A hallway!" she replied.

The knob gave a haughty sniff. "Wrong. Don't be so literal."

With an impatient sigh, she held her palms close together, trying to imagine they were walls that had adventures between them. Hearing footsteps just then, she turned to see Prince Foulsmell coming down the hall. He was holding his Handbook open and reading what . . . school rules? Class assignments? Or a story . . . like maybe an *adventure* story? The two sides of the Handbook's cover . . . weren't they kind of like walls?

She looked at the knob, unsure. "Is the answer 'a book'?"

Snick! The goose head turned back into a regular brass knob. She'd been right! After pushing through the library door, Snowflake paused in the *C* aisles for cheese, crackers, and cashews for herself. Then another stop in Section *D* for dandelions and dill to feed the bunny. And lastly in Section *F* to grab a book of Hans Christian Andersen fairy tales.

However, when she got back to her room, the bunny was nowhere to be found. She searched high and low. Finally, she heard a soft, little sneeze. A small feather floated out from the lowest part of her bed.

Getting down on her hands and knees, she peered at the bottom mattress. There was a hole in it! The bunny had burrowed inside it and made himself a snug home.

"Come on out," she called gently. "I brought you something to eat."

She set the dandelions and dill in a dish by the entrance to his new burrow. Not waiting to see if the bunny would come out to eat, she climbed up on the top mattress. Munching cashews, she opened the fairy-tale book and began to read "The Snow Queen."

After a minute or two, she heard the bunny thump across the floor to begin munching his dinner, too. A bit later, she heard scrabbling sounds. She glanced over the side of the mattress and saw that the bunny was running circles around her bed.

Abruptly, he stopped and did the weirdest thing. *Boing!* He executed a wacky jump-twist movement that sent him straight up in the air. Upon landing again, he went racing around and around the bed a few times more, boinging every now and then. At the top of his boings, the tips of his ears reached as high as the mattress she was lying on. The sight caused her to roll with laughter, and she put a hand over her mouth to stifle the sound, just in case Ms. Goose (or anyone else) was nearby.

"You want to come up?" she asked the bunny, since it seemed clear he was trying to reach her with all those boings. The bunny gazed up at her as she went down and picked him up. After setting him on her mattress, she climbed back up. He snuggled against her side as she lay on her stomach and went on reading. He was good company, she decided. And she could certainly use a companion now that she was going to have to keep to herself as much as possible.

"This is the tale of 'The Snow Queen,'" she read aloud to him in a soft murmur. "It's about a girl named Gerda who has lots of adventures. You don't really hear much about the Snow Queen even though the tale is named for her. The main stuff she did is try to make Gerda's friend — a boy named Kai — go live in an evil castle where he had to move puzzle pieces around forever and ever." She patted the bunny. "It's a pretty weird story. Interesting, though."

She flopped over on her back, and the bunny hopped onto her stomach. *Oof!* When she decided to let him stay, he grew bolder. He put his head under her hand and gave it a nudge.

"Are you telling me you want to be petted?" she asked, feeling a little tug at her heart. Naturally, he didn't answer. But she petted him, anyway. "I have to warn you that I might be evil," she admitted to him. "I might be as dangerous to you as Wolfgang or Dragonbreath. Or worse even." She hoped not, though, because she couldn't stand the thought that she might accidentally do something to hurt this sweet bunny.

"Unfortunately, "The Snow Queen" tale does feel like it fits me," she whispered sadly. "Still, I don't exactly *feel* evil. Guess that doesn't mean I'm not, right?" After all, since she could cause ice and snow to form, it seemed highly probable that her magic had caused the strange sleet on the island earlier. Sleet that might be responsible for the glazed looks and out-of-control emotions that had beset Mary Mary, Cinda, and other students. *Gulp!* What if her evilness was catching somehow?

Maybe the principal and Ms. Jabberwocky had suspected

she was the Snow Queen all along. Had they only been wait-ing for her to confirm their suspicions? Would she soon be kicked out of the Academy for causing trouble, like what had happened at her last school?

"Maybe, but I'm here now," she murmured to the bunny. They burrowed under the covers together. She really liked this little fuzzy-eared guy. If she got kicked out, would she be able to take him with her? No, that wouldn't be fair to him. He needed a safe, permanent home, and who knew where she'd wind up?

For this bunny's own good, she needed to find him a new caretaker — and fast. Tomorrow, she would ask around again. Even though it would break her heart to give him away.

14

Gone

When something cold brushed Snowflake's nose the next morning, she opened her eyes to see a bunny face barely an inch away from her own. She was lying on her side in bed, and the bunny was sitting on her pillow, staring at her. He was also munching on the end of the green hair ribbon she was wearing.

"Hey, little Kai," she said. "I mean, little *guy*." She'd accidentally called him the name of the boy who was Gerda's best friend in "The Snow Queen." The bunny's ears perked up.

"Oh, you like that name?" she asked him. It was a cute name and kind of suited this critter. Still, *ugh*, she didn't want to think about that fairy tale right now. It was the cause of all her troubles! Besides, this was Saturday. No school. She should try to forget about being an evil character for a while and just have fun.

She pushed herself up on one elbow and pulled the ribbon from her hair. Looping it around the bunny's neck, she tied it in a loose bow. "You are grimmadorable!" she told him. As if to say he agreed, the bunny did some cute nose twitches and ear wiggles, which sent her into giggles.

When she started to sit up, she bumped the top of her head. "Ouch! Hey! Our room is smaller today. About half normal size, don't you think?"

Snowflake knew that the library could expand or shrink whenever it wanted to, but this was the first time she'd seen it this small. She slid out of bed and set the bunny on the floor. It was hard to squeeze around the bed and get dressed with so little floor space in the room.

Since the bunny seemed eager to go exploring, she took him along to Section C and got breakfast for them both there. She found carrots and clover for him and cereal for herself. Then she ate sitting in a chair while the bunny ate on a small carpet at her feet. She also grabbed a cloak to wear in case she went over to Ice Island later.

"Ms. Hagscorch is scary, but her food is way better than this boring stuff in the library," she remarked to the bunny as they ate. (He was an excellent listener.) "But we can't go back to the Hall. The more I hang around with other kids, the more chance I might do evil to them. Or befriend them and get my heart broken when it doesn't work out and they start to not like me." Exactly what had happened at her last school after the albino bees episode. She sighed. "So this is how it has to be. For me, anyway. We'll find you a good home soon, though, I promise."

Noticing movement out of the corner of her eye, she straightened. Something was flying up the *C* aisle toward them. The snowflake wand! Jack Frost was following right behind it. He executed a few flips in midair and landed on a shelf across the aisle from her on top of a box labeled CRUMBS. Yeah, that was perfect, she thought. Because it was totally *crummy* that he had come around again!

As for the wand, it got so overexcited at finding her again that it accidentally dunked itself in her cereal bowl before it could put on its flake brakes. Startled and damp now, it pulled back out and shook off the droplets of milk that clung to it.

Snowflake tossed the wand onto the shelf beside Jack Frost. She didn't want any part of an evil wand. When she didn't acknowledge his existence, Jack Frost picked up the wand and started marching up and down the shelf, twirling it in one hand like it was a baton and he was a majorette. When she ignored him some more, he straddled the wand like a horse and began riding around and around her.

Spotting the bunny, he flew to eye him curiously. "Who's this?" he asked.

Uh-oh! She shrugged as if the bunny meant nothing to

her. Because if she showed she cared about him, Jack might try to find a way to use that information to help himself.

"Just some random bunny," she said. "He hopped over from the *B* section, so I gave him a carrot." Unfortunately, the bunny chose that moment to leap into her lap and nudge her hand to ask for a pat.

"Seems rather fond of you," Jack Frost observed. He leaned forward. "Hey! What's around his neck? Isn't that your hair ribbon?"

Oops! He'd caught her. It *was* her ribbon, of course. "Yes, the ribbon's mine, but he's not my bunny," she insisted. "I'm only trying to find a home for him is all."

"Mm-hmm." Jack cocked his head so the tassels on his cap dangled sideways. She couldn't tell if he believed her or not.

Meanwhile, the wand was acting restless. It bucked up and down till Jack tumbled off. After righting himself in midair, he managed to grab hold of it. Then, without warning, he flipped it toward Snowflake. It plummeted dizzily end over end until it landed in her cereal bowl again.

Milk splashed everywhere this time, splattering both Snowflake and the bunny. As she hopped up and set the bowl on a shelf, the bunny leaped off her lap. "Would you please just . . . *chill*!" she yelled at Jack, her voice going up on the last word.

Oh, no! She'd gotten upset, and now that thing that had happened in the principal's office was happening again. The bunny froze in midleap! And a pair of geese that had been flying by overhead carrying net bags full of artifacts froze as well in midair. Unfortunately, Jack Frost was unaffected.

Looking pleased with her, he bounded closer. "You've got talent! Good thing your 'chill' magic doesn't affect me, since I'm already naturally frosty."

"You made me mad on purpose, didn't you?" Snowflake accused.

He snickered. "Just a little test. And you passed with flying colors. As I suspected, you're very much like the GA principal. Your talent is strongest when you get all riled up. Look at what you were able to do!" He gestured toward the geese poised in stillness above them.

"How do I control my 'talent,' though?" she asked desperately.

"Why would you want to? It's frostastic!"

Just then, the chill started to wear off. Still half-frozen, the geese began to plummet.

"No!" she shouted in horror. Seeming to sense her need, the wand zipped into her hand. She waved it at the two geese overhead. "You *will* un*chill*!"

In the nick of time, the geese unfroze completely. They flapped their wings, soared higher, and continued on their way. Having avoided one disaster, Snowflake turned to check on the bunny. Unchilled now, it executed one of its weird fruit-loopy *hopposite* corkscrew jumps, and then shot off down the library aisle heading higher in the alphabet.

"Wait! Come back here, bunny!" she yelled, sprinting after him. Good thing the library was way smaller today because that made the aisles shorter. She was way up in the alphabet, in the *L* section, lickety split.

There were *lots* of students in the L aisles today. Most seemed to be looking for long johns. And when she got to Section *S*, there were students looking for scarfs and sleds. Probably hoping to have a last bit of fun over on Ice Island. Now that the sleet storm was over, the island would be safe — until it melted.

She asked everyone she passed, but no one had seen the bunny. Eventually, she reversed direction and ran back to the *B*s in case he had filed himself there. No such luck.

The library had shrunk enough that she could see all the way to the front of it from the *B* aisle where she stood. Given the number of students going in and out, she wondered if her bunny could have hopped out the library door when it was open. It would be grimmawful if she lost him, even though she knew she couldn't continue to keep him forever. What if he got hungry later or wanted his chin rubbed? Would whoever found him know that he didn't like having his ears messed with? Or that when he wiggled his whiskers, it meant he was hungry?

While heading through the *B* section, Snowflake almost bumped into Prince Dragonbreath. He was in the process of demonstrating his fiery breath for some other boys. Startled at the sudden blast of fire, she gave a shriek and backed away, shaking.

"Don't act like that," he pleaded, his green eyes earnest. "I have feelings, you know. And I swear I won't hurt you or anybody else around here. I might be in the *B* section, but I'm not a *bad* person."

Not a bad person. Unlike her, if Jack Frost was right. "Sorry, but I can't help it," she blurted. "I'm scared of fire!"

He looked surprised. "Why?"

"It's dangerous. That's why!" she exclaimed.

"Anything's dangerous if you misuse it. Like, if someone's not careful they could slip on your ice," Dragonbreath countered. "But ice is also fun, right? Just like fire can be a good thing, useful for cooking and heating."

He had a point.

"And anyway, fire is something I do. Like you do ice and snow. I can't change that. It's part of who I am. Like I said, it doesn't make me a bad person. So don't be afraid of me, okay?"

Suddenly, and without warning, a great sadness filled her. "Well, maybe you should be scared of *me*. Because I really *am* a bad person."

His eyebrows rose. "What? I don't believe that."

"Well, you *should*!" Snowflake's lower lip began to tremble, and she had to blink back tears. Feelings of frustration welled up in her until finally, unable to control them, she yelled, "I think I'm the Snow Queen!"

Dead silence fell around them. At first, she thought she'd frozen everyone again. But then a goose flew by overhead, and she realized the other students in the library had all gone still of their own accord, flabbergasted at her admission. Ms. Goose glanced up from her tall desk near the door and sent her a look of sympathy. Or was it *pity*? Whatever it was, Snowflake didn't want it. Embarrassed by her ill-timed outburst, she dashed out of the library.

She couldn't do anything to take back her words, but maybe she *could* find her bunny. Worry grew in her as she scoured the school halls and classrooms for him without success. Eventually, she took her search outside, thinking he might have gone back to munch flowers in the Bouquet Garden. She hoped Mary Mary hadn't caught him and taken him to those hunters!

Once in the garden, she beckoned softly, "Little Kai, where are you?" The first time she'd called him that name had been a mistake but he'd perked up, so maybe he would come if he heard it now. When the bunny didn't appear, she stood in the sunshine and heaved a discouraged sigh. "This day is really going downhill. First, losing Kai, and now my island is probably melting away under this bright sun."

She heard footsteps coming up behind her and ducked down. She didn't want to talk to anyone. But it was too late. Mary Mary had found her.

"What are you and your magic charm doing in my garden?" the contrary girl demanded, frowning suspiciously.

"Charm?" echoed Snowflake, getting to her feet and glancing around. She hadn't brought her wand.

Mary Mary pointed toward a flower bush nearby, and Snowflake saw that it was loaded with bouquets of chrysanthemums. And something else, too! Her wand had found her and stuck itself in the bush, trying to blend in and pretend its snowflake tip was a blue-white mum.

Giggling a little, Snowflake went over and reached for it. Just in time, she remembered it was probably evil and snatched her hand back. Too bad, because she had enjoyed doing magic with it and had been starting to like having it around.

"I suppose you think you're better than me just because you have a charm now," Mary Mary griped. "It's not like you found it or anything. Rumor is that it found you. Which is *so* not fair. There are lots of us — *lots of us* — here at GA who should have gotten our charms before you." The glaze-eyed girl swiped her hand in the air and whacked a few blossoms off the bush closest to her.

Whoa! Mary Mary was acting super mad! Snowflake was seized by her usual desire to flee from all this drama, but she also wanted to get to the bottom of what was going on here. Because, though she'd only known Mary Mary for a week, this didn't seem like ordinary contrariness.

Ignoring the urge to bolt, Snowflake leaned toward the garden girl and set a hand on her arm. "Do you feel okay?"

Mary Mary brushed her off. "I'm fine! And so is your dumb Ice Island for your information. I heard it hasn't melted a drop. Which is really weird if you ask me!" With that, Mary Mary stomped off toward the Once Upon River.

Snowflake followed her to the riverbank and looked across to her island. It was covered with students all having fun. What Mary Mary had said was true! Even though the sun was blazing overhead, the ice castle and the island it stood upon looked as strong and sturdy as they had yesterday when she'd made them. Why weren't they melting at least a little?

Then she noticed something under the toe of her slipper, and gasped. It was her hair ribbon, lying on the riverbank.

"What's wrong?" asked Mary Mary, watching her pick it up.

Snowflake held out the green ribbon. "That bunny was wearing this a little while ago in the library. So he must have come this way. Have you seen him?"

With an irritated shake of her head, Mary Mary said, "He's not in my garden. I watered everything a little bit ago, and he would've come out." She studied the ribbon in Snowflake's hand more closely. "Why is that thing all glittery? Looks like it's covered with sugar."

"Huh?" Snowflake brushed the ribbon with a fingertip. "No, it's *frost*." An icy tingle ran down her spine. Had Jack Frost taken her pet to the island? And maybe left this as a clue so she'd follow? What was he up to?

She looked at Mary Mary. "I think Kai has been bunny-napped!"

"Who's Kai?" asked Mary Mary.

"My bunny!" Snowflake called back as she ran for the last empty swan boat docked on the bank.

"What makes you think anyone would bother with that pesky flower muncher?" Mary Mary demanded, following her. Before Snowflake could explain further or climb aboard the large boat, Goldilocks, Red Riding Hood, and Rapunzel also arrived at the dock.

"What's wrong?" Goldilocks asked, seeing Snowflake's alarmed expression.

"I think my pet bunny may be over on the island!" said Snowflake. She held out the ribbon. "A bunny-napper — I think it might be Jack Frost — took this off him. I found it on the riverbank." She heard herself say *my pet bunny* and knew that by using those words she was admitting just how much she cared for little Kai. She'd given up pretending that she didn't care because her heart told her that just wasn't true. She had to find him and make sure he was okay!

The girls piled into the boat. Snowflake wasn't sure why Mary Mary decided to come, rather than return to her garden, but she figured Kai could use *all* the girls' help.

When they arrived on the island, their footwear instantly transformed to skates like it had the day before. They glided away from shore and soon came across Cinderella and Rose. The two girls were waving their arms around and busily trading angry insults.

"Skating in a figure *nine*? What a dumb idea!" Snowflake heard Cinderella say.

"Well, why does it always have to be an eight? You're the dumb one," said Rose.

Snowflake and the other girls watched in stunned silence as the bickering escalated. Soon, Rose and Cinderella were yelling nose-to-nose.

"Ha! I think you are totally dumb-*not*-tastic," said Rose.

"Well, same to you and even more, so there," said Cinderella.

Mary Mary skated up to the angry girls. But instead of trying to calm things, she shouted, "Well, I think you're both double-dumb-dumb idiots!" Her words inflamed the two girls further, and they started to shout insults at Mary Mary, too.

Snowflake frowned. All this friendship drama was having an effect on her. It was making her upset! *Uh-oh.* With a huge effort, she managed to keep her temper under control. For the moment, anyway.

"Stop fighting!" Red Riding Hood shouted at Cinderella, Rose, and Mary Mary after finally finding her tongue. Good advice, but Snowflake knew it sometimes wasn't that easy.

"Yeah, what is wrong with you guys?" demanded Rapunzel, looking between the three arguing girls.

"See how weirdly glazed their eyes look?" Snowflake began. "I think —"

Just then, Red Riding Hood wailed, "Ow! Something stung me!" She rubbed at a pink mark on her wrist.

Snowflake glanced up at the sky. Just like yesterday, sleet had begun falling. When she looked back at Red, she saw that the girl's eyes had taken on the same glazed look as the eyes of the three arguing girls.

"Hey, Cinderella!" Red called out suddenly. "I just heard Prince Awesome say he likes Rose now instead of you. And Mary Mary, Wolfgang told me he thinks your flowers are ugly."

Of course, this false gossip caused more hurt feelings and led to more arguing. What a mess!

"I don't know how you're causing this, but I like it. Good job!" said a voice near Snowflake's ear.

She whipped around to see Jack Frost. "You mean you're not doing it?" she demanded. Putting a hand on one hip, she wagged a finger at him. "And where's Kai?"

"Huh?" the sprite asked in surprise.

"My bunny. You took him. I know you did. And I bet you're causing all this, too," Snowflake accused, gesturing toward the uncharacteristically bad-tempered girls.

"Am not." Jack huffed a frosty puff of air. "As for your bunny, er, Kai, you should be thanking me. I saw him hitch a ride here to the island in a boat with some other kids. So I pulled off his ribbon and left it behind as a clue for you. And don't worry, last I saw, Dragonbreath had him."

Snowflake gazed around skeptically. "Oh, really? Where are they, then?"

"Maybe they're in the castle, or maybe he took the bunny back across the river. I don't know, but I'm telling you the truth."

That was a relief about Kai being with Dragonbreath. Because now that she'd gotten to know the boy a little better, she wasn't worried he'd hurt her pet, not really. Well, maybe still a little bit worried. She narrowed her eyes at the sprite. "And you're really not causing all these arguments?"

"Not my handiwork," Jack said, shaking his head emphatically. "I thought it was yours."

"Mine? Nuh-uh." But even as she denied it, she wondered anxiously if she *could* be the cause of it and just didn't know it. Did evil work that way? Out of the blue, some sleet zinged toward her. Snowflake cried out and recoiled. But for some reason, the sliver of sleet stopped short. And just for a sleeting, er, *fleeting* moment she saw her reflection in it as if she were looking in a mirror.

Instead of striking her, the sleet backed away and went over to strike Goldilocks instead. Weird! Was she immune to sleet because of her snowy, icy powers, in the same way Jack Frost wasn't affected by her "chill" magic because of his frosty powers?

"That sleet isn't sleet at all," Jack Frost declared now, confirming Snowflake's own dawning suspicion. "It's pieces of reflective glass."

All at once, things became crystal clear to Snowflake. "I think I know what's happening!" she exclaimed. "While you were inside that snow globe in Principal R's office last Thursday, I broke Ms. Wicked's favorite mirror. Then some kind of magic — maybe hers or the E.V.I.L. Society's — whooshed the mirror's broken pieces out the window. I think the sleet is actually those glass shards. The evil in them is glazing everyone's eyes and causing them to fight!"

"Frostacular!" Jack Frost said, rubbing his little hands together in sprite delight.

Ignoring him, Snowflake attempted to wave all the students into the castle for protection. But by now, many on the ice had been sharded, and they were all too busy arguing and yelling at one another to pay attention to her.

It seemed that only she, Rapunzel, and Snow White still had their wits about them. She had to get those two Grimm girls to safety. "Into the castle! Let's try to figure out a plan before the shards get you, too!" As she herded them into the castle, she explained about the "sleet" having come from Ms. Wicked's broken mirror.

Once inside, the three girls were surprised to see some trolls in Troll Moving Company uniforms. "All finished," the head troll informed someone. He was talking to Jack Frost! Apparently the sprite had slipped into the castle before the girls.

"Hope you don't mind. I had them do a little redecorating to add more *shine* to your lair," Jack informed Snowflake after the trolls tromped outside.

"Stop calling it that!" she hissed at him. Rapunzel and Snow White were looking at her with confused expressions, obviously wondering why she might need a lair. Snowflake pretended not to notice their confusion since she didn't want to explain. These girls hadn't been in the library earlier and didn't yet know her fairy-tale identity.

"Oh, no! Look!" Snow White exclaimed, drawing her attention. She was turning in a circle and pointing at what was hanging on the icy walls around them. "I've seen these before. They're . . ."

As she paused, Snowflake and Rapunzel followed her gaze. Their eyes went wide when they saw what she was pointing to.

"Ms. Wicked's mirrors!" all three girls chorused together. Everywhere they looked, mirrors were either leaning against or hanging upon the castle walls. Jack Frost must've had the trolls bring the mirrors from the library and install them here for what he'd called "shine."

Snowflake stared at the mirrors, aghast. *"Nooo!"*

15

Puzzling

Other unwanted changes had been made to her castle, too, Snowflake noticed. She anxiously went to check them out with Snow White and Rapunzel at her side, and Jack Frost not far behind. There were lots more walls than she remembered. They divided the castle into dozens of little rooms, each hung with mirrors. And there were doors and stairs that led to nowhere, spiky tangled railings made of thorns, and statues of scary, fantastical creatures all made of ice that leered at them.

"It didn't look like this yesterday," Snowflake assured Snow White and Rapunzel. "I would never design something so wicked."

"Think the evil from my stepmom's mirrors transformed things?" Snow White whispered as they ventured deeper into the castle.

"Or some other kind of evil," Snowflake said, eyeing Jack Frost suspiciously.

"It wasn't me!" he protested. "I only had the trolls bring over the mirrors." Then he added slyly, "But if these mirrors brought their evil with them, maybe you could harness it. You might be able to use it to keep building on this castle forever. I'm talking new wings and new halls that would never melt. Permafrost! The sky's the limit, seeing as how you're the Snow Queen."

Hearing this, the other two girls sent her startled looks. Snowflake groaned inwardly. She wished Jack hadn't gone and blabbed about her identity. She'd wanted to explain to them about it later on when things calmed down.

"I'm pretty sure what he says is true," she told the girls quickly. "But don't worry, I'm not going to suddenly act all evil." She glared at the sprite.

Jack Frost sighed. Then his eyes rounded as the sounds of scraping and crunching reached them. More weird statues, thorn railings, and strange stairs were forming in the ice on all sides of them. Gruesome gremlins, ghastly ghouls, and creepy monsters all grinned or scowled at them from the walls around the mirrors. The girls huddled up, studying their surroundings with frightened faces.

"Where's your wand?" Rapunzel whispered to Snowflake. "Can't you use it to change things back to however they were yesterday?"

"Yeah, because this is creepy," muttered Snow White.

"Last time I saw that wand, it was pretending to be a chrysanthemum in the Bouquet Garden," Snowflake replied. "I left it there."

"Why?" asked Rapunzel, sounding surprised.

Before Snowflake could explain that the wand was likely as evil as Ms. Wicked's mirrors, she spotted something in the distance up ahead. A bright light was casting a strange shadow across the castle floor. It looked like two giant fingers held up in a V-shaped peace sign.

"What's that?" Jack Frost shrieked. He ducked behind the girls.

The shadow crept closer and closer. The girls scooted back in fear, ready to run if they had to. Who knew what kind of horrible creature might have fingers that huge? Finally, the fingers came into view. Only they weren't fingers at all. They were ears. Tall bunny ears casting an unusually long shadow!

"Kai!" Snowflake cried out in delight. She ran toward her missing pet, her arms open wide. She scooped him up and snuggled him. The bunny seemed thrilled to see her, but soon he started wriggling to get down. When she set him on the floor, he immediately did one of his crazy boings and took off back in the direction he'd come from, moving toward the bright light.

"Wait! Where are you going?" Snowflake raced after him.

"I think he might be trying to show us something," said Rapunzel as she and Snow White caught up.

The girls, with Jack Frost tagging along, had to hurry to keep up with the speedy bunny. Along the way, random shards drifted around them in the air like some kind of floaty indoor sleet. They managed to dodge the shards at first.

However, eventually Snow White stopped short. She jerked and grabbed her elbow. "Ow!" she wailed. "Oh, this is grimmorrible! I think I've been sharded. I —"

Catching her reflection in one of her stepmother's mirrors, she moved closer to gaze at herself. "Whoa! I'm sooo beautiful," she murmured, turning this way and that to view her reflection. Then she spoke to the mirror:

"Mirror, Mirror, don't you think
That I'd look cute all dressed in pink?
Although of course you know it's true
That I do shine when wearing blue."

She went on and on, admiring herself and inviting the mirror to do the same. The shards had affected her differently than some of the other students, but still in a *negative* way.

"Ha-ha! She's as vain as Ms. Wicked now," guffawed Jack Frost, doing gleeful flips in the air.

"It's not funny, Mr. Frostypants," Snowflake snapped. "She can't help it. It's the shard's fault. We have to help her!"

"The best way to do that is to end whatever is causing this evil," Rapunzel reasoned. "I say we catch up to your bunny and see what he wants to show us."

"I guess you're right," Snowflake agreed after a moment. "Maybe that's our best hope for now. We'll come back for Snow White after we break the mirrors' spells."

Though they were reluctant to leave their friend, the two girls continued on with Jack Frost at their side. When they finally entered a room at the heart of the castle, they didn't see Kai at first. Because it was bright enough in there to need sunglasses!

Mirrors hung all around them on every wall, reflecting rays of sunlight beaming in from the heart-shaped windows Snowflake had made in the central tower above. And these mirrors were way scarier than those in the other rooms. Wavery images of otherworldly, menacing-looking creatures with sinister faces, pointy noses, clawed fingers, and wiggling hair were reflected in all of them. Remembering their History class studies, the girls could guess what the creatures were.

"Those things in Ms. Wicked's mirrors," Snowflake whispered to Rapunzel in horror. "They've got to be Dastardlies from the Nothingterror. I bet they're trying to enter Grimmlandia through these mirrors!"

Rapunzel nodded grimly. "Maybe I can use my magical comb charm to cage them if they actually get out." But as she reached into her pocket for her charm, she cried out sharply. "Ow!" She pulled her hand out to touch her shoulder. "Oh, no, I think I've been struck by a shar —!"

Her words dwindled away before she could finish. As her eyes glazed over, she flipped her long, dark hair over one shoulder. Frowning at Snowflake, she said crossly, "This castle should be mine, not yours. You have no need for such a big space, but I could live here with my cats!" She wandered off then, muttering to herself about the unfairness of things.

Jack Frost giggled. "I think your goth friend has gone a bit green around the edges."

"Jealousy," Snowflake whispered. Another negative emotion. She frowned at Jack and added, "Not her fault. Those shards have a bad effect. Now help me find my bunny."

"Grrr!" growled a low, strong voice. The sound was coming from a thick cloud of mist at the far side of the room.

The sprite stared at the mist. "What was that?"

"I don't know," Snowflake whispered.

"Let's go see," Jack said, sounding excited. Snowflake wanted to run away, but that wasn't an option. She had to be brave and discover what the bunny had led them to see. Maybe it would somehow save her friends, er, acquaintances, from the evil that had befallen them. Or were they friends now? Things were getting confusing.

"Who's there!" she called out in a firm voice. No reply. Though scared, she stumbled into the fog cloud, trailed by Jack Frost. Around them, wispy strands of mist swirled, turning into clawed hands or evil faces with fanged smiles now and then before changing back into fog. When the mist suddenly disappeared, Snowflake stopped still, a chill sweeping over her.

Because there on the ice, only ten feet ahead of her, sat a huge green monster — perhaps a Dastardly! Her snowflake wand lay on the ice beside the creature. But what horrified her most was the sight of Kai perched calmly on its shoulder.

Had the wand flown here to wait for her? If so, had the Dastardly captured it? And Kai? Or maybe the wand really was evil and was here to take part in whatever rotten plan was unfolding.

"What's that green guy doing?" Jack whispered to her. "Playing a game?"

Snowflake shrugged uncertainly and moved sideways to get a better look. There was an oval game board about four feet long and three feet wide lying on the ice in front of the monster. Covering its surface were hundreds of sharp, flat glass shards. She watched as clawed green fingers dragged and placed the shards within the game board's metal frame, as if they were puzzle pieces. There didn't seem to be enough shards to complete this puzzle, however. She had a feeling she knew where the rest were, though. Off striking other students and changing their personalities!

"That's no game board," she hissed. "It's the frame from the mirror Ms. Wicked escaped through to . . . wherever she went. I took it to the library after the glass inside it broke."

Jack nodded carelessly. "Those trolls must have brought it here."

"I also think that green guy might be a Dastardly. And he's trying to fix that mirror. Please, can you fly over and bring me my wand before he sees us?" she asked Jack. Even if her charm *was* evil, she desperately needed its magic to rescue her bunny before he became Dastardly dinner!

"Why should I?" Jack replied, folding his arms as he lazily flitted around her.

Thanks a lot! she thought. Any warnings to this flighty sprite about the dangers of repairing an evil mirror would probably do no good. He'd be happy if *more* evil entered Grimmlandia!

"I thought you wanted to be my sidekick," Snowflake countered, knowing that might be the only way to get him to act.

"Now you're talking!" he crowed. He zoomed off toward the wand. However, another mirror flew off the wall and blocked him like a shield, or a sprite-swatter. *Smack!* He slammed into it and fell to the ice, looking dazed. More mirrors began to fly off the walls, positioning themselves around the room like an army hovering in midair. Were they awaiting orders from that Dastardly?

Without warning, it looked up and spotted her. Her breath caught. Was she about to be destroyed?

But right away the creature's red eyes turned to sparkly green and its scaly green-skinned body twisted and shrunk till it had shape-shifted into a boy wearing a tunic, breeches, and boots.

"Hey! A dragon boy!" shouted Jack, still sounding a little dizzy as he sat up from the ice where he'd fallen.

"Dragonbreath?" Snowflake whispered, recognizing him at last. "What are you doing?" Had he been sharded, too? Like that boy in her tale, was he now trapped in this castle, doomed to move puzzle pieces around forever? She shivered.

"Snowflake! Sorry about shifting. I took dragon form to ward off possible trouble. I guess you've noticed the weird creatures trying to get out of the other mirrors?" He looked up at her briefly, then concentrated on his task again.

"Yeah. Dastardlies trying to enter this realm from the Nothingterror?" she guessed, watching his hands work on the shard puzzle. When he nodded, she didn't add that she had thought *he* was a Dastardly at first, too. She was glad he was back to his normal self now.

Just then, Kai hopped off the boy's shoulder and boinged over to her. She picked him up and hugged him in relief.

"I found your bunny on the island, and when I saw some trolls bringing mirrors into the castle, I followed to see if you were in here," Dragonbreath informed her all in a rush. "After that, everything started getting weird and changing around here, and when I noticed some mirrors flying into this room, I came to check things out and found this broken one."

"It belonged to Ms. Wicked," Snowflake put in, moving closer to stare at it.

He nodded. "I think it somehow controls the other mirrors and they're waiting for its orders."

Snowflake's eyes went wide. "Then why are you fixing it? Stop!"

Before he could reply, disembodied voices began crooning to them. "Yes, stop. Give up, give up." The voices were coming from the Dastardlies in the rest of the mirrors, which still floated around the room looking ready . . . for battle?

Cocking his head toward them, Dragonbreath replied to her earlier question, saying, "That's why. Those other mirrors don't want good-hearted characters like us to put this thing back together. And I'm thinking that maybe that's because, in our hands, it could become a tool for good."

So this boy still thought she was good, even after she'd told him who she really was back in the library?

As Dragonbreath set another shard in place within the frame, the voices crooned, "Nooo."

Maybe his theory was right. She'd heard enough about Ms. Wicked and the E.V.I.L. Society's connection to the Nothingterror to know they longed to take over all of Grimmlandia.

Snowflake threw off her cloak and made a makeshift bed for her bunny to lie on nearby. Then she kneeled beside the broken mirror, picked up some shards, and reached out to add them to the puzzle.

"Good idea! These mirrors were probably hoping for someone evil to come along and repair this thing," Jack Frost noted, hovering just over her head. Instantly, Snowflake snatched her hand back. Was she the evil they were awaiting?

"He's wrong. You can help. You're not evil," Dragonbreath assured her.

She shook her head, uncertain. "There aren't enough shards here to finish this thing. But I think I know where the missing ones are."

"You do?" Dragonbreath asked eagerly. "Can you use your wand to summon them here?"

"Maybe." Could she trust her wand, though? It seemed she had no choice if they wanted to complete this mirror puzzle.

She raised her hand, and called out, "Wand, please come, and —" But the enthusiastic wand didn't wait for her to finish speaking her rhyming command. It jumped up and whooshed toward her. Halfway across the room, it changed direction. As if drawn by some unseen magnetic force it spiraled backward until . . . *smack*! It stuck like glue to a mirror hung so high on the wall that there was no way Snowflake could reach it. The wand spun in circles against the glass as if trying to wrench itself free, but to no avail.

"I think that evil mirror is trying to take my wand into the Nothingterror!" she cried in horror. She was staring up at her wand and trying to figure out how to get it back, when she heard Dragonbreath let out a yelp. Fearing the worst, she turned.

He was lying flat on his back on the floor. "I slipped on the ice," he explained.

"Are you okay?" she asked. "Here. Let me help . . ." But before she could reach down and try to pull him to his feet, a dozen long shards rose from the mirror he'd been trying to put together. She gasped as they hurled themselves at him. However instead of striking him, they attacked his clothing, driving themselves through the outer edges of his tunic and breeches like stakes, effectively pinning him to the icy floor.

She dropped down beside him and tried to pull the stakes out. When that proved impossible, she did the only thing she could think of. "Shape-shift!" she urged him. He looked at her uncertainly.

"What are you waiting for?" she asked.

"I don't want to scare you," he told her.

"You won't, I promise. Do it!" she insisted. It was a lie, of course. She was terrified of dragons!

Within seconds, Dragonbreath did as she asked. His body turned green and scaly and began to grow into dragon shape. *Ping! Ping!* One by one, the shards pinning him popped from the ice like corks from bottles. After they flew into the air, they clattered to the ice floor. Snowflake gathered them and replaced them in the mirror puzzle.

When next she dared peek, Dragonbreath's tail had unfurled to a dozen feet long. His dragon body was covered with green scales.

"Frost-awesome!" enthused Jack Frost upon seeing him shift into a powerful monster again. When she scowled at him, he ducked his head and muttered, "Or maybe not?"

The Beasts and Dastardlies in the mirror cackled with laughter. The sound echoed throughout the room, causing Snowflake to tremble. She glanced at the dragon warily. With its red eyes, it looked nothing like the boy she knew. Why didn't Dragonbreath shape-shift back to boy-size now that he was free? What if, in his dragon form, he'd forgotten all about her and his quest to save the realm from evil? What if he'd forgotten he was good?

Backing away now, she called to Jack Frost. "Please, please fly up and try to rescue my wand from that mirror holding it captive."

Jack flipped his muffler around his neck and crossed his little arms. "This time I want to know what's in it for me."

Without thinking, she said, "Helping good triumph over evil?"

"Why would I want that?" Jack asked in surprise. "No, I want a reward."

"Okay. I'll think of some way to reward you later," she promised. "Wand's honor."

The sprite sighed. "Oh, all right." He headed for the mirror. When he was only inches away from it, he reached out a hand to grasp the wand. "Ow!" From out of nowhere, a shiny, tiny shard struck him.

Forgetting all about retrieving her wand, his lips curled into a sneer and he began circling the room high overhead. "Those Grimm brothers thought they were so smart, collecting their tales. Well, what about me?" he groused loudly. "They couldn't include me in even one single story?"

As he circled the room thinking darker and darker *negative* thoughts, he worked himself up into such a fury that he began to bounce off the walls. *Boink!* "I'll get my revenge, though. One day, I'll rule the entire realm of Grimmlandia!" *Boink!* "Soon, it'll be payback time, Grimm dudes!" *Boink! Boink!*

This was a troubling development. The shards must be more potent in this mirrored room than they were elsewhere. If Jack could be struck and affected in here, maybe she could, too. And Dragonbreath. Snowflake looked around warily. They needed to get out of here, fast.

"Hey, Dragonbreath!" she called. But the enormous dragon just stood there on the icy floor. It was so still that for a moment she wondered if she'd somehow accidentally "chilled" it. But then she saw its tail twitch and its eyes swivel to watch Jack's fuming antics. What was it thinking?

All the room's mirrors followed the dragon's gaze and turned themselves toward Jack too. While they were distracted, the dragon quickly reached up to the high mirror that had trapped her wand. With the flick of one clawed, scaly green finger, the wand was wrested free from the mirror's surface. Wasting no time, Snowflake's charm flew straight to her and settled into her hand. So that's what Dragonbreath had been doing — trying to divert the mirrors' attention away from her wand!

"Change back, so we can make a plan," she called to him. No answer. He must not be able to respond to her while in his dragon form. And now there was new trouble brewing.

The mirrors in the room were angry. Deciding Dragonbreath was more powerful than she, they faced off against him. They flew off the walls and surrounded the dragon. As if under a spell — and perhaps Dragonbreath was? — he made no attempt to defend himself.

As much as Snowflake might want his help, it looked like everything was up to her now. She needed a plan to foil that mirror army. And fast!

Her fingers curled tightly around her wand. "If you're truly a good magic charm, you'll protect us," she told it. Quickly, she waved it over Ms. Wicked's broken mirror and said a rhyming command to call back the missing shards.

"Fly to me, shards,
From far and near.
Land on this mirror
And fit yourselves here!"

There was a wild, whooshing sound. Within seconds, shards began zooming through the windows into the room. Joining together, they whirled in a tornado shape like the one she'd seen in the principal's office earlier that week. One by one, they dropped lower and fitted themselves neatly into the golden frame.

But when this formerly-wicked mirror was remade, would it turn out to be an evil one, a good one, or something in-between?

While the shards kept coming, Dragonbreath — still in dragon form — continued to stand, twitching his tail slowly back and forth. The floating mirrors crowded closer and closer to him, an evil army about to attack. He was outnumbered! Still, he was a powerful dragon. He must be holding off for fear that she and Kai, and maybe Jack, too, would be harmed if there was a battle.

Knowing she had to act, Snowflake instructed her wand to watch over her bunny. Then she took a fortifying breath to prepare her for what she was about to do next.

"Yoo-hoo! Look out, you Dastardlies," she called. She picked up a chunk of ice and hurled it at the closest mirror. In a flash, the mirror angled toward her, repelled the ice chunk, and sent it hurtling back toward her!

Whoa! She ducked just in time to avoid being struck and the chunk smashed into the ice floor behind her. *Crack!* A rift in the floor opened so suddenly that she had to windmill her arms to keep from falling backward into the freezing cold river that flowed beneath the ice. "Help!" she cried out. At the last minute, she regained her feet. *Phew!*

A change had come over the dragon at her cry. Now it gave a tremendous roar that rocked the room, making the mirrors sway and almost causing her to accidentally topple backward again.

Roarr! Zzzt! A great blast of fire shot from the dragon's snout. Fire slammed into the mirror Snowflake had been aiming for and a half-dozen others nearby. They melted!

"Way to go!" she cheered. She was so relieved she almost forgot all about her fear of fire.

Her words seemed to encourage the dragon, and it trained its fiery breath on another group of mirrors. *Roarr! Zzzt! Roarr! Zzzt!* More mirrors melted.

But then Snowflake noticed something worrisome. The mirrors weren't the only things melting around here. Under the heat of his flames, the floor was melting, too. There were great cracks all around her now in addition to the one she'd almost fallen into. Cracks that were getting wider by the second. Some were even traveling far across this room and beyond.

Although she wasn't much good at architectural structure yet, she *did* know that without a sturdy floor, the castle would eventually crash in upon itself. Her stomach clenched with fear. They had to best these Dastardly mirrors and get out of here. And fast, or they'd soon be cast into the river below! Though she could swim, she knew for a fact that dragons could not. And even if Kai could swim, the river might prove too wide, deep, and cold for him.

Zzzt! Roarrr! The dragon melted the final mirror just as the last shard fit itself into the frame on the floor.

Immediately, as if it were the mirrors' magic that had prevented him from transforming into a boy again, Dragonbreath shifted back to a prince.

"Let's skedaddle!" Snowflake grabbed her wand and Kai. Dragonbreath grabbed the gold-framed mirror puzzle and leaped to safety just in time to keep from falling into one of the ever-widening cracks in the floor.

But the melted mirror lumps weren't so lucky. They slid through the cracks and sank into the river. *Glub, glub, glub!*

16
Good or Evil

Snowflake and Dragonbreath raced for the castle exit. All around them, the castle began to break apart as the cracks in its floor widened and lengthened. There were way too many now to repair.

The two friends ran on, winding their way outward from the center of the collapsing castle. Soon, they met Rapunzel and then Snow White. Both girls looked dazed, but the evil spells on them had lifted now that all the shards had returned to the broken mirror, and they gleefully joined Snowflake and Dragonbreath to dash the rest of the way out of the castle.

At last, the four of them emerged onto the skating rink. And just in time.

CRUNCH! CRASH! Behind them, the castle fell into ruin. Snowflake hugged Kai in her arms, grateful they were safe. "You okay?" she murmured to him. As if in answer, the bunny nudged her hand, seeking a pat. She smiled and obliged.

There were dozens more students still outside on Ice Island. They wore concerned and surprised expressions as they gathered around the foursome, asking all sorts of questions. Snowflake quickly explained how shards from Ms. Wicked's magical splintered mirror had been the cause of so many of them becoming argumentative. When Dragonbreath tried to give Snowflake all the credit for saving the day, she explained that it was he who had melted the mirrors.

Cheers went up. "Hooray for Dragonbreath and Snowflake! Fire and ice saved the day!"

Snowflake checked the eyes of those around her. None were glazed. The shard spell had truly lifted from one and all. And that was something to cheer about!

As some of the students began leaving the island to row back to the Academy, Dragonbreath turned to Snowflake. "Did I scare you?" he asked her, nodding toward the castle. "All that firepower, I mean."

She shrugged. "To tell you the truth, I was so determined to beat those mirrors that I kind of forgot to be scared."

He laughed. "Good." He glanced over at her castle. It was now unrecognizable, a great jumble of partially melted blocks. "I'm sorry about your castle," he said, his voice taking on a serious tone again.

"It's okay. I'll rebuild it even better," she assured him. Then she grinned. "And maybe you can help? Turns out dragon fire is not only great at carving out windows and doors, it can also melt and reshape ice." At this, Dragonbreath's green eyes sparkled happily. He really was cute, Snowflake decided. And more important, he was nice.

"You got it," he replied. "So, we're friends?"

She smiled up at him. "Friends," she agreed softly.

"Hey, does anyone else hear a squeaking noise?" Prince Foulsmell asked, looking around at the dozen remaining students. They all stopped talking to listen.

"It's coming from there," Prince Awesome called, pointing to a beach ball–size lump of ice on the ground near the castle. They all went over to check out the lump.

"It's Jack Frost!" exclaimed Snowflake. "He's trapped inside the ice!"

"I can't melt the ice around him," said Dragonbreath, shaking his head. "I might accidentally fry him."

"Listen, I think he's trying to tell us something," said Snow White.

They all leaned closer to the lump of ice. "Other side," Jack Frost croaked. Misunderstanding, the group moved to the other side of the ice lump.

"No!" Jack squeaked in frustration. Somehow, he managed to turn his gaze to Snowflake's wand. "Other side," he repeated.

She looked at her snowflake wand in confusion. But

doing what he seemed to be asking, she turned the stem in her hand and flipped the wand over. She saw at once that its reverse side had changed. Instead of a snowflake, it was now a sun! After she showed it to the other students, she touched the sunny side of the wand to the ice lump. And the ice encasing Jack magically defrosted!

"Well, it's about time!" groused the sprite, leaping out. Without a single word of thanks to Snowflake for freeing him, he shot high in the air and whizzed out of sight.

She wondered where he was off to or whether she'd ever see him again. She really hoped he'd given up on the idea of becoming her sidekick at least!

Soon, the remaining students headed for the swan boats. Snowflake climbed into a six-seater. Rose, Rapunzel, Cinderella, Red Riding Hood, and Mary Mary got in with her.

On the way back to the Academy, Snowflake suddenly blurted, "I've already told Rapunzel about this, but the rest of you should know that I've discovered what tale I'm from." She took a deep breath, and then admitted, "I'm the evil Snow Queen." To her surprise, no one chucked her out of the boat!

"Yeah, we all know that already," Mary Mary informed her. "Lots of people overheard you say it in the library before they came out to the island and . . . well . . . word gets around, you know?"

"For a while, some people thought *I* was evil," Rose put in, as if trying to reassure Snowflake. "My fairy tale got rewritten to make me look bad. But once Ms. Wicked escaped through her mirror, my tale rewrote itself back to its original state and proved I wasn't evil after all."

"I don't think my tale is going to rewrite itself," Snowflake told her sadly. "I think I might actually have a bad side. When I get upset, my feelings kind of spiral out of control."

"So?" said Rapunzel, dipping an oar in the river. "Everyone loses their temper once in a while."

"I know," said Snowflake. "But when I lose mine, bad things happen." She explained to them about the albino bees and about chilling people and animals into statues. "The only time I feel like I'm really in control of my powers is when I'm holding this," she said, touching the wand that lay next to Kai in her lap.

"You know, I think charms are meant to help us harness the magic already within us," Cinderella told her. "I've always been a terrible dancer, but now my glass slippers help me boogie down. I found that out at Prince Awesome's ball my first week at GA. Still, I think that somewhere inside I already had the ability to dance. It took my charm to bring that ability out."

"And I used to be afraid of heights — still am, really — without my charm." Rapunzel pulled her magical comb from her pocket. It was a deep, rich, polished black, and its spine was carved with fanciful wild plants. "The longer I have it, the less afraid I feel. I think it may actually be helping me get *over* my fears."

"Yeah, my basket gave me the confidence to act onstage," said Red Riding Hood as she paddled. "Well, that and some tricks Wolfgang taught me for overcoming stage fright."

"So you really think my magic charm might help me control my temper and keep me from becoming evil?" Snowflake asked, feeling hopeful.

All five girls nodded. "I say evil is as evil does," said Rapunzel.

"Exactly," Mary Mary said. She looked at Snowflake. "You may have the power to do evil, but you try to use your powers — both the icy kind and the melty kind — for *good*."

"She's right. Truly evil people don't *break* evil spells and take care of bunnies," Rose added.

Snowflake picked up her wand and flipped it from side to side. Snowflake. Sun. Snowflake. Sun. Two sides to her nature, perhaps? The important thing was to not let her upsetting emotions or bad temper overshadow her sunny side. It was food for thought, at any rate.

Once they arrived at the Academy, the girls went to the office to tell the principal all that had happened. Principal R was glad all was well, but bemoaned the loss of Jack Frost. "Now who's going to spin the straw?" he wondered aloud.

Remembering what Jack Frost had revealed to her — that he'd only *tricked* the principal into thinking he needed help to spin gold, Snowflake made a suggestion. "I have a feeling that if you try to make some gold all by yourself again, you might find that you can."

Principal R's eyes lit up as if he sensed she knew something he didn't. He sat and worked at the spindle to see what would happen. But nothing did. "Bah! I told you I needed Jack's help." His cheeks reddened with frustration at his inability to produce any gold by himself.

"Try again . . . Principal *Rumpelstiltskin!*" Snowflake said, using his full name on purpose. Everyone gasped. But she just waited calmly for the inevitable temper fit to start. Sure enough, the principal flew into a tizzy on the spot. It did the trick! In a mad fever now, he fed the straw and stomped the pedal as the spindle whirled in a blur.

"Look! You did it!" said Ms. Jabberwocky, pointing at the pile of gold he'd created.

The principal's anger drained away at the sight. He beamed, then asked, "But how?"

"You were actually the one who was spinning it into gold before," Snowflake explained. "Jack Frost told me it was your anger that gave you the power. He just pretended to help."

"Makes sense now that I think about it. Because I'm angry in my fairy tale, right?" said the principal.

"Yeah!" Ms. Jabberwocky laughed and let out a stream of fire. After being around much fiercer blasts from Dragonbreath, Snowflake didn't even flinch!

A few minutes later, when the students filed out of the office, Snowflake wound up next to Mary Mary. They were the last to leave, and since no one else would hear, Snowflake used that moment to fess up. "I've been hiding out in the library," she confided. "Sleeping there I mean."

Mary Mary came to a halt outside the office doorway and looked back at her in surprise. "Why?"

"Because I thought you liked your alone space and didn't really want to share a room with me," Snowflake explained.

"Well, I do like to spend *some* time alone . . . but . . ." Mary Mary paused as if searching for just the right words.

"Yes?" prompted Snowflake.

"But not *all* the time," Mary Mary admitted.

It was now or never, thought Snowflake. She would risk getting hurt feelings in order to find out the truth of the matter. "Well, does that mean you're willing to give it try — the roomie thing, I mean?"

"Yes, yes!" said Mary Mary. Then she added shyly, "I might not be the easiest roommate, though. You'll be surprised to hear this, but sometimes, I can be a bit contrary."

The fact that Mary Mary thought no one had noticed this about her made Snowflake want to smile. So she did, saying, "I guess neither of us is perfect. Which is *perfect*! Let's do it!"

They started to head off, but stopped when a small voice behind them let out a groan. The girls whirled around. Jack was back!

"Erg. I can't stand it," he said, levitating in midair. "All this *good*ness. *Bleah!* Get me outta here!"

"If you don't like it, why'd you come back to the Academy?" Snowflake asked him.

Jack Frost looked at her in surprise. "For my reward, of course!"

Principal R burst out of his office. "What makes you think you deserve a reward?" he demanded, having overheard. "You *tricked* me! I didn't need your help to spin gold at all!"

"Oh, that. I . . . uh . . . I . . ." stuttered Jack.

It was the first time Snowflake had ever seen him at a loss for words. Feeling a bit sorry for him, she spoke out on his behalf. "Jack did try to help when things went wrong at the ice castle. But he got sharded and couldn't."

"Exactly!" said the sprite. "That's what I meant to say."

"Oh, all right. Fine," Principal R told Jack reluctantly. "You can have a small reward. What is it you want?"

"Really?" Perking up, Jack Frost zoomed down to hover in front of the principal's nose. "I want to be a puppet master, pulling the strings of some evil puppets. I want to rule!"

The principal tapped a finger on his long chin. "Hmm. Evil puppets. I can make your wish happen if you promise you will confine your troublemaking to the place I send you. And you must only do small evils and never hurt anyone good."

"Squee!" Jack twirled around in delight.

"It means going back in the snow globe," the principal informed him.

Jack stopped twirling and his shoulders sank. "Not squee."

"Only briefly," the principal assured him. "Just to launch you to your new home. I'll even send a recommendation letter saying that you were too evil for us, so we kicked you out of the Academy. That should convince someone to be your evil puppet. Deal?"

Jack Frost did a happy triple air flip. "Deal!"

17

Jack Frost

Thump! Something sailed over the great wall that surrounded the realm of Grimmlandia and dropped to the ground in the Dark Nothingterror.

Three Dastardlies gathered around and stared at it. "Hey, lookie. It's a square stone," said one of them.

Actually, it was a round ball of glass. A beach ball–size snow globe to be exact. But Dastardlies were not all that bright. A moment later, Jack Frost burst out of the crack in the globe and looked up, up, up.

These Dastardlies were giants. No problem! He could fly. He zoomed high to look the creatures in their eyes. Each only had one of them, right in the middle of its forehead.

"Whatter yoo?" one of them asked. "Some kind of bug?" The other two guffawed and tried to swat Jack.

"Stop! I have a letter from the principal of Grimm Academy testifying that I am extremely evil," he announced. He whipped it out to show them.

"Huh?" they said. "Can't read. What's testerfrying mean?"

"Perfect," Jack Frost muttered gleefully to himself, tucking the small, rolled-up letter away. He hadn't known what to expect from the Nothingterror when the principal had revealed where he was going. Still, this place agreed with him so far. These Dastardlies might be big and strong, but a smart guy like him could trick the pants off them!

"The letter is to tell you that from now on, you are my bosses," he explained patiently. "Which means, I'll tell you what to do so you don't have to ever think again. You just do as I say." He gave them a big, wide smile as if this were great news for them.

Actually, it didn't really make sense. But as Jack had hoped, the Dastardlies got so excited about the idea of being bosses that they didn't seem to notice that the rest of what he'd said was not in their favor.

"Dohkay," grunted the biggest of them. The other two nodded.

Jack Frost smiled. Ah, he was looking forward to life in the Nothingterror with his evil puppets. It was going to be *frostastic*!

18

Emerald Tower

A few days later, Snowflake ran up the Academy's twisty stairs, holding her snowflake-sunburst wand in one hand and a sheet of paper in the other. She screeched to a halt where the stairs dead-ended at two doors on Pink Castle's sixth-floor landing. One door was emerald green, and the other was pearly white. Without pausing, she shot through the emerald one and dashed across the outdoor stone walkway that ran between the girls' three dorm towers. She heard splashing in the multitiered fountain down below in the courtyard between the fifth-floor dorms.

"Hi, Mermily!" she called out, without bothering to look over the stone railing. Because who else would be splashing around in the fountain but Cinderella's mermaid roomie? Sometimes she even slept there overnight.

Sure enough, Mermily's bubbly voice drifted up to her a couple of seconds later. "Hi, back, Snowflake!"

Up ahead, the pointy top of Snowflake's dorm, Emerald Tower, gleamed like a jewel in the sunlight. When she reached its door, she burst inside. Then she zoomed past its central common area and over to the alcove she now shared with Mary Mary. Whipping the curtain door aside, she practically danced into their room.

"I aced the History test!" she announced, hopping around in excitement.

Mary Mary looked up from her desk. There was an unusual expression on her face — a slight twist to her mouth. If you'd never met her before, you might have mistaken it for a grimace, but Snowflake was getting to know her better. And for Mary Mary, this was a look of happiness. Happiness on Snowflake's behalf.

"Wow! Congratulations," Mary Mary told her, leaping to her feet. And there was real warmth in her voice.

"I couldn't have done it without you and everyone else," said Snowflake. Her new GA friends had all helped her study. Their help, plus the Handbook's tips about test-taking anxiety, had done the trick.

At this, Mary Mary broke out in an actual smile! To Snowflake's surprise and pleasure, the girl went over to their window and leaned out. "Guess who aced her History test?" she yelled.

Snowflake popped her head out of the window alongside her roomie's in time to see a volley of marshmallows go flying. Mary Mary had been calling to some girls who were outside atop the long narrow courtyard that ran the length of the flat rooftop above the auditorium. With Cinderella's assistance, Rapunzel was doing a test run on a small-scale model of a catapult she and Snowflake had designed in Sieges class. Which explained the flying marshmallows. Beyond them, Red Riding Hood, Snow White, and several others were playing putt-putt golf.

Gleefully, Snowflake waved her test paper at the girls. (Naturally, they were too far away to see the big fat *A* at the top of it, but still.) "Thank you, guys, sooo much for helping me study!"

At this, all the girls cheered. "Woot! Woot!" "Grimm-awesome!" "Knew you could do it!" "Way to go, Snowflake!"

Cinderella cupped her hands around her mouth. "Hey!" she called up. "If we had some snow outside on the lawn we could go sledding to celebrate!" Then she added, "Hint, hint."

"Your wish is my command!" Snowflake called back. Though the glass-slippered girl was no longer sharded and grumpy, she had decided she still preferred to be called by her full name instead of the nickname Cinda.

However, no way did Snowflake want to be called Snow Queen! She was glad the secret of her identity was out, though. In a sense, learning who she was and the reason she had the power to freeze stuff had sort of unfrozen *her*. Yes, she was the Snow Queen, but there was a warm feeling inside her nowadays. She might be an evil character in her tale, but in real life, her character was much more complex. And, luckily, the Academy students seemed to understand and accept that. There was no need to keep apart from others. She loved having lots of friends!

Now she waved her wand toward the lawn below Pink Castle and chanted:

"Bring snow fun
For everyone!"

Instantly, big fat flakes of snow began to come down, falling only on the Pink Castle lawn.

"Yay! Meet you guys outside!" Red Riding Hood called up. She and the others below scattered to go to their rooms for jackets, scarves, and mittens before racing outdoors. When other students noticed the snow, word was sure to spread and lots of students would join in the sledding. The more, the merrier!

Turning from the window, she saw that Mary Mary was already at her armoire getting her cloak. Feeling happy, Snowflake let her gaze sweep their room. She loved everything about it, from their raised canopy beds, with swooping swags of pretty see-through fabric draped across the tops, to their desks and chairs, which sat beneath those high-built beds.

As she grabbed her own cloak and her wand, she wondered how Jack Frost was getting on. Word had it that Principal R had sent him to the Dark Nothingterror. Since the sprite delighted in evil, that was probably the perfect place for him. And Grimmlandia was undoubtedly a little safer without him.

Just then, Snowflake's bunny hopped into the room and did one of his crazy corkscrews before zipping under her desk to snuggle in the bed she'd made for him there. She and Mary Mary giggled. Kai's chew toys were scattered around her desk and throughout the whole of Emerald Tower, because he was basically allowed to roam as he pleased. All the girls in the dorm adored him and shared in his care. And Mary Mary often took him to her garden to play these days, though certain bushes remained off-limits.

"Let's go! Let's go!" Mary Mary urged.

Snowflake slipped on her cloak, then she and Mary Mary made for the door. Suddenly, both girls stopped in their tracks. Because a little piece of paper had just floated into Snowflake's hands from out of nowhere. She read the words on it aloud: "Ice Architect." She looked at her roommate in confusion.

Mary Mary gasped, her eyes lighting up. "It's your tower task!"

Hearing that, Snowflake whooped with joy.

"C'mon! Let's tell everyone," she said to Mary Mary, and they raced out of the dorm. As her roommate dashed ahead, Snowflake paused on the outdoor stone walkway to gaze out at the river. Ice Island still glistened there, frozen as ever.

Ideas for all the new things she could build on the island swirled in her head like flakes in Jack Frost's snow globe. A gigantic ice slide, for example. And a new ice castle. Maybe she would design this one so students could safely skate in through one of its doors and out another. She was Ice Architect now, after all. It was her official tower task! Which seemed proof that her island was destined to become a permanent — as in never-melting — landmark at Grimm Academy.

She now truly believed that what Rapunzel had said was true. *Evil is as evil does.* So she was determined to channel her evil powers toward good forevermore. Having accepted that her wand really was her magic charm — a *good* charm, and that such charms only came to those who were good of heart, she knew she was up to the challenge.

Hearing a gleeful shout from the first sledders below, Snowflake did a happy little twirl on the walkway, then dashed off to join them. She could hardly wait to turn Ice Island into a year-round winter wonderland fun park where students could skate, build snowmen, sled, and have parties in the new ice castle she would create!

It was going to be absolutely grimmawesomely, grim-mazingly snowtastic!

Check out the next Grimmtastic Girls adventure!

From the authors of
Goddess Girls–your
Grimmtastic
fairy-tale adventure awaits!

Read the whole
Grimmtastic series!